o?

I unfolded the paper in my lap and instantly recognized Salvador's handwriting.

Dear Elizabeth,
   I know you're really mad at me right now, but I just want you to know that the only reason I'm sort of acting like I'm going out with Anna is because I don't want to hurt her feelings. You know what a bad time this is for her, and I think if I broke up with her, she'd just be all alone. I can't do that.
   But when things get better with Anna, I want you to know that it's you I want to go out with. It's you I've liked all along.

Love,
Salvador

Don't miss any of the books in SWEET VALLEY JUNIOR HIGH, an exciting new series from Bantam Books!

Cheating on Anna

Written by
Jamie Suzanne

Created by
FRANCINE PASCAL

BANTAM BOOKS
NEW YORK・TORONTO・LONDON・SYDNEY・AUCKLAND

RL 4, 008-012

CHEATING ON ANNA
A Bantam Book / September 1999

*Sweet Valley Junior High is a trademark of
Francine Pascal.*

Conceived by Francine Pascal.

*Produced by 17th Street Productions,
a division of Daniel Weiss Associates, Inc.
33 West 17th Street, New York, NY 10011.*

ISBN: 0-553-48666-7

Published simultaneously in the United States and Canada

*Bantam Books are published by Bantam Books, a division of Random
House, Inc. Its trademark, consisting of the words "Bantam Books" and
the portrayal of a rooster, is Registered in the U.S. Patent and Trademark
Office and in other countries. Marca Registrada. Bantam Books, 1540
Broadway, New York, New York 10036.*

PRINTED IN THE UNITED STATES OF AMERICA

OPM   0 9 8 7 6 5 4 3 2 1

To Johnny Boulton

Anna

"So, what did you do today?" Salvador del Valle asked me—*again*. It was Sunday night, and we were having another one of our boring, awkward phone calls, the kind we'd been having all week.

"Not much," I answered. I didn't want to tell him that I'd been staring at my computer screen all day. Writing and rewriting the same poem over and over. I didn't want Salvador to think that I'd lost my mind. "I just hung out in my room."

"It was really sunny. The Doña wanted to play Frisbee, but we couldn't find one," Salvador said. The Doña was Salvador's kooky grandmother. His parents were in the military and traveled a lot, so Salvador lived here, with the Doña.

"Oh," I answered. I couldn't think of anything else to say. What were we talking about anyway? Nothing.

"Well, I'd better go finish my homework," I said.

"Me too," Salvador answered. Then he hesitated. "Is everything all right, Anna?" he asked.

"Yes," I answered, surprised. "Fine."

"Okay. Well . . . see you tomorrow," Salvador said. "Sleep well."

"You too. Bye."

"Bye."

I hung up and stared at the words I had written before Salvador called, so crisp and formal on my computer screen.

> *I Wish*
> Every time I pass your room
> I wish I heard your music
> Blaring loud.
> Every time I watch TV
> I wish I felt your hand
> Grab the remote.
> Every time

Yuck.

It was garbage.

Garbage that I'd spent all day trying to write.

I love to write, especially poetry. My English teacher had even suggested that over spring break I go to a special creative-writing camp for teens in Lake Tahoe. The application was due in the mail any day now.

But lately my mind had been wandering—I

couldn't focus. And everything I wrote sounded stale and stupid.

I moved the cursor to the first word. My finger hovered over the keyboard.

Then I pressed down the delete key and held it.

One by one, the letters of my poem disappeared from the screen, like one of my grandmother's crocheted afghans unraveling into a ball of yarn. Till at last the entire poem had been unwritten. Gone. Totally erased from the universe.

I stared at the blank screen, the cursor blinking, waiting for me to write something.

I started again. *Death* . . .

My eyes watered as I stared at the word. Then I typed control Z—undo. The word instantly disappeared.

I sighed. Our principal once told us in an assembly at school, "Your life's a novel, and you are the author."

Yeah, right. If only.

If only I could edit out all the horrible, unwanted parts of my life as easily as I deleted stupid poems from my computer screen.

Then my big brother, Tim, would still be in his room next door, annoying me by playing his hip-hop CDs too loud. Chasing me down the hall to tickle me for calling him lamebrain. Hiding my shoes before school in the morning right before the bus came and refusing to tell me where they were unless I promised to make his bed and be his slave for a whole week. Being totally obnoxious. And totally the best ever brother in the whole wide world.

Instead of lying cold and dead in a cemetery beneath a pot of ridiculous plastic lilies.

I shoved my chair back from my desk and got up to look out the window. The full moon cast a surreal glow on our backyard, and everywhere I looked, I saw reminders of my brother. The cement driveway where he'd helped me learn to ride a two-wheeler. Our tree house, where we'd hidden from Mom and Dad when they called us to do chores.

The moon had been full that night too, exactly a year ago, when we got the call. A teenage boy coming home drunk from a party had slammed into my brother's car head-on. The other kid had stumbled out of his car without a scratch, they said.

Ambulances raced Tim to the hospital, and he was already in surgery by the time we got there. But nothing could save him. Not the doctors' skilled hands. Or my father's assurances. Or my mother's prayers. Or my tears. I always thought that after a while people just got over someone dying. That was before it happened to me.

I know now that you're never over it. It doesn't go away or get better. It just changes you. It becomes a part of who you are—Anna Wang: Black hair. Petite. Korean heritage, good grades . . . dead brother.

Sometimes I wake up and think, *It's not true!* It's a mistake. Or a dream. Or a weird, cruel joke, like when a prankster sends you pizzas you didn't order or when you accidentally get someone else's mail.

I keep imagining a plot twist, like the strange, convoluted ones they dream up on soap operas when they want to revive a character they killed off but now want back in the story line. . . .

The doorbell will ring, we'll all race into the living room, and Tim will waltz in the front door, smiling like always, and explain that it was all just one big, horrible mistake. . . .

I'm never going to be over it. It's not like a sore throat that gets better. Or a broken arm that heals. Or a bad haircut that grows in.

I let the curtains drop and sat back down at the computer. I reached for the keyboard and rested my fingers lightly on the keys, like on a Ouija board, looking for answers.

There's so much I want to say. But just then the words wouldn't come. With a sigh I shut down my computer. Too bad I couldn't use a few swift keystrokes to shut down my feelings as well.

Call Sal back, I told myself. *He's your best friend. Talk to him. He'll listen. He'll understand.* I reached for the phone. But just then I heard someone knocking at the door. My mom poked her head in. "Are you ready for bed, Anna?" she asked me. "It's late."

"It's only nine-thirty," I said, hoping she'd take the hint and go away.

But she didn't. "I brought you some warm milk," she said as she shuffled into the room.

"Some *what?*" I asked, incredulous.

She stared back at me, her eyes rimmed with dark circles that never seemed to disappear. A year ago her hair would have been perfectly combed, but now it was a mess of tangles and fly aways. Her pink bathrobe hung open, revealing the white flannel nightgown she wore day in and day out.

"Warm milk," she repeated. "My mother used to make it for me when I was a little girl. It will help you sleep." She set the cup and saucer down on my nightstand, then took me by the shoulders. "Come on. Bedtime!"

"But Mom, I—"

"No arguments. You'll get sick if you don't get your rest. It's almost flu season, you know."

There was no point in arguing. I stood up and climbed into bed.

My mom plumped up my pillows, then

tucked the covers around me like I was a small, sick child. A lot of kids wouldn't have found this unusual at all. But I did.

My mother used to work as a nurse in a hospital. She was always very organized and into time management, trying to keep her work schedule and home responsibilities running smoothly.

But after Tim died, she just totally lost it. She took a "long vacation" from her career that had stretched from "a month or two" to nearly a year. Now I wondered if she would ever go back.

For months she did nothing. Really nothing. I'd come home from school and find her still in her nightclothes. Or not find her because she'd have locked herself up in her room, crying. Things were left undone. My dad worked longer and longer hours, so sometimes I had to do stuff, like make dinner or talk to the plumber.

Dad said we needed to give her time.

But just this past week or so, it was like Mr. Hyde had turned into Dr. Jekyll. It was like she suddenly remembered she had another child too, and she wouldn't leave me alone. As if taking extra-good care of me would somehow make up for not being able to protect Tim from that drunk driver.

But it felt weird—wrong somehow. Like the whole time she was mothering me, she was thinking of him.

Anna

At last Mom stopped fussing and brushed my forehead with a kiss. "Good night, sweetheart," she said dreamily.

As soon as she wandered back out into the hall, I jumped up and closed the door, then got into bed again. I reached for my phone. Salvador's line was busy. "Thanks a lot, Sal," I said into the receiver, as if he'd done it on purpose.

I turned off the overhead light, leaving on the little lamp on my nightstand, like I always do. I thought it might be good to just fall asleep and forget about everything—Tim, my mother, homework. . . .

But it was Salvador I couldn't get out of my mind.

Salvador and I have been friends since kindergarten. We'd shared so much. And now things had changed.

Since the first anniversary of my brother's death was coming up, I've been really upset lately—missing Tim and feeling lonely. Last week Salvador came over to talk. He was so sweet. He put his arms around me and just let me cry and tell him stories about Tim. And then—out of the blue—he kissed me.

And it actually made some of the hurt go away.

I was totally surprised.

I mean, I'd never really admitted to myself that I could like Salvador as anything more than a friend. And I'd always kind of suspected that he had a big crush on Elizabeth Wakefield. Ever since the first day of school this year, we'd been sort of a threesome. Best friends, inseparable.

Elizabeth has been really great, listening to me talk about Salvador—it's nice to finally have another girl to talk to.

And it just seems so right that me and Salvador should be more than friends. Sure, it's kind of weird—like on the phone tonight. We're not sure how to act now that our relationship has changed.

On the first day after the kiss, when I saw him at school, I was really nervous, and Salvador was kind of shy and awkward, which he never is!

I started to give him a kiss on the cheek at his locker, but we knocked heads instead—not very romantic. And Salvador blushed, which he never does either.

But I guess that's to be expected when a friendship changes like this. When it develops into something . . . else.

It will get better once we get used to it, I thought. *Going out with Salvador is going to make everything better.*

I'm so lucky to have Salvador.

And Elizabeth too.

I don't know what I'd do without their friendship.

Salvador

I feel like I'm cutting class.

I glanced over my shoulder. The first-period bell hadn't rung, I wasn't due in English yet, and the halls swarmed with kids laughing and talking and slamming locker doors. Technically I was a free man. I was right where I was supposed to be.

So why did I feel like I was about to get caught?

Because I was trying to avoid Anna Wang.

Anna, my best friend since kindergarten. Now my . . .

Say it, Salvador, I told myself.

My *girlfriend.*

It was just too weird.

Don't get me wrong. Anna's the greatest. She's the smartest, nicest, cutest girl I've ever known, and I really care a lot about her. She's like the sister I never had.

But I'd never even thought about her as a girl—I mean, not like a girl I'd want to *date.* I mean, no offense.

And nothing *happened* for me when we

kissed. Nothing like whenever I even *look* at Elizabeth Wakefield—major fireworks, like the Fourth of July.

So how did a guy find himself going out with his best girl *friend* instead of the girl he dreamed of being his *girlfriend*?

I'm still not sure how things got so messed up. I thought *Elizabeth* and I were going to be together. I've already kissed her *twice!* And we had planned to tell Anna all about it. But when Elizabeth went to her house to finally tell her, Anna was crying about her brother. So Elizabeth chickened out and just comforted her.

Then *I* went to see Anna to tell her about me and Elizabeth, and she looked so amazingly sad. So I did what any best friend would do—I held her in my arms and let her cry her eyes out. And then somehow, before I knew what had happened—I must have totally been out of my mind!—I had kissed *her* too.

This might have been funny in the movies. But in real life, it was a total disaster. I was in way over my head.

After our kiss Anna went totally girlie on me and turned the whole episode into this major romantic thing. I mean, Anna is my best friend, and usually when she's happy, I'm happy. But this was too much and *all wrong*. Before I knew what had hit me, Anna and I were . . . a couple. She even called Elizabeth and told her all about it! You can imagine how Elizabeth took that! She's pretty much stopped talking to me.

Can't she see that I don't *want* to be Anna's boyfriend?

It's just that I have no choice! I'm stuck.

I can't break up with Anna. She's so sad right now with everything that's going on at home—she needs me. And there's absolutely no way she can ever find out that I kissed Elizabeth. That would ruin everything.

Crunch!

I was spacing out and bumped right into somebody. Their books crashed to the ground. "Sorry—," I said, and turned around to pick up the books.

My heart stopped. It was Elizabeth, my Wonder Girl, on her way to English too.

I reached for a book, and our hands touched. Did she feel it—that electric current humming from our fingertips?

Our eyes met. She's got these amazing blue-green eyes. And my insides turned to jelly.

A beautiful blush stained Elizabeth's cheeks, and my heart swelled. *She still feels the same way about me!* I thought, and I wanted to kiss her again. Which, of course, I couldn't. Not there on my knees in the middle of Sweet Valley Junior

High. I wanted to say something to her—tell her it would all work out.

But what could I say?

"Elizabeth . . . ," I began.

She looked away and quickly began to gather up her books.

"Elizabeth, listen—"

"Hi, guys!"

Elizabeth and I jerked apart. *Anna!*

Elizabeth scrambled to her feet, dropping half her books again.

I gathered them up and got to my feet. "H-Hi, Anna."

It's not like we'd been doing anything wrong, but my face was burning up.

Anna didn't seem to notice how weird Elizabeth and I were acting. She just smiled at us and slipped her arm through mine. Then she stood on tiptoe and gave me a quick little kiss on the cheek.

I could feel my face turn even hotter. I glanced at Elizabeth.

Did I imagine it? Or did I see her wince?

Man—I hoped my face wasn't as red as hers. How could Anna not notice?

"You guys have got to help me," Anna said. "I'm having an awful time with my writing. I was trying to write another poem for *Zone* last night." She put her hand on Elizabeth's arm, while her other arm was still linked with mine.

Talk about a love triangle!

I could tell Elizabeth was struggling to act super-normal for Anna's sake. *She's so cool* . . . , I thought.

"—you, Salvador?" Anna stared at me.

"Huh?"

Anna laughed. "Forget to eat breakfast this morning?"

I shrugged.

"I just asked Elizabeth to help me with my piece at the *Zone* meeting this afternoon. You're going to be there, right?"

"Sure," I said.

Zone was the alternative 'zine we were starting up—Anna, Elizabeth, me, and our friend Brian Rainey. We had all started out on the school newspaper, the *Spectator*. But the paper didn't print the kind of stuff we wanted to write or *read*, for that matter. So we'd gotten money together by selling advertising space to local businesses and created *Zone*. We were almost ready to print our first issue, and we were all pretty psyched.

"Well, I'll see you guys later," Elizabeth blurted out suddenly, and before Anna or I could say anything, she'd dashed off down the hall.

"Where's she going?" Anna wondered.

It was a good question. Elizabeth and I both had Mrs. Bertram for English first period. I

14

guess it looked pretty weird for her to go ahead without me.

"Maybe she has to talk to one of her teachers," I suggested lamely. "So," I said, turning back to Anna, trying to make conversation. "Did you have much homework last night?"

"Um, no." But then suddenly Anna froze. "Oh my gosh!" she exclaimed. "My science homework!" Her brown eyes looked up at me in horror. "I forgot all about it! Can you help me do it? Quick, before the bell!"

That's a switch, I thought worriedly. *Anna always does her homework.*

It made me so sad to see my best friend under so much strain. I'd do anything for Anna. Anything. I know she'd never ask, but she could copy my homework every day if she wanted.

I dug into my backpack for my homework, and she dragged me to a bench in the hall. We have the same teacher at different times, and the homework was the same. I did my best to help her, even though I wasn't sure I really understood it.

And as she frowned studiously at my bad handwriting, I studied her face—so serious and fragile and tough at the same time. I couldn't possibly break up with Anna. I couldn't hurt her like that.

I was just going to have to ride this thing out—at least for now.

15

Elizabeth

I sat by the window in the empty classroom, hoping it would fill up before Salvador arrived. From now on I had to be more careful to avoid him. At this point I could hardly stand the sight of him.

It was hard enough going to school every day, knowing that Salvador and Anna would be there. Together. A couple.

And Anna had absolutely no clue that Salvador and I had kissed. *Twice*.

When my twin sister, Jessica, and I were re-zoned from Sweet Valley Middle School to Sweet Valley Junior High, I had been skeptical about making new friends. But on the first day of school I'd met Salvador and Anna and all my fears disappeared. They were funny and smart and into the same kind of things I'm into. It's hard to say what attracts certain people to certain other people, but I knew I'd found two good friends.

Then Salvador had messed everything up by liking me and kissing me.

And *I'd* messed everything up by liking him and kissing him back.

And then Salvador had ruined our friendship forever by kissing *Anna*.

The damage was done.

He was such a jerk!

But it wasn't like I could tell *Anna* that.

She's been so sad lately about her brother. Going out with Salvador seems to have sort of cheered her up a little.

The only thing I could think of to do was to completely avoid them both.

A few people began to trickle into the classroom. Out of the corner of my eye I saw Salvador's dark, curly hair and bright blue shirt. I took out my English notebook and began flipping through the pages, staring at the words without seeing them. I could feel him approaching. Finally he sat down in his assigned seat, just two desks away. Mrs. Bertram came in the room and put her books down on the big desk at the front of the classroom. I kept my eyes focused on the little gold *x* she had pinned to her blazer. She began to talk, but I had no idea what she was saying—I was too busy not looking at Salvador.

It was going to be a long class.

All of a sudden the boy next to me, David Arnaut, yawned and stretched and sort of thrust his fist at me. He was trying to pass me a note, I realized. I brushed my pencil onto the floor and bent down to pick it up, snatching the folded square of paper from David's hand on my way up.

I unfolded the paper in my lap and instantly recognized Salvador's handwriting.

Dear Elizabeth,

I know you're really mad at me right now, but I just want you to know that the only reason I'm sort of acting like I'm going out with Anna is because I don't want to hurt her feelings. You know what a bad time this is for her, and I think if I broke up with her, she'd just be all alone. I can't do that.

But when things get better with Anna, I want you to know that it's you I want to go out with. It's _you_ I've liked all along.

Love,
Salvador

I felt queasy, and I shut my eyes, sucking in air. My hands were trembling as I grabbed my pencil and turned to a clean page in my notebook. I

could feel my face getting redder and hotter as I
scribbled a note back.

Salvador—
  Don't think I'll be waiting for you.
  You're a liar. I would never go out
with you, not in a million years.
  Anna deserves better.
                              Elizabeth

Carefully I tore the scrap of paper from my
notebook and scrunched it into a ball. I glanced
to my right and caught Salvador watching me,
the corners of his mouth turned up in an eager
little smile. I looked down and tossed the ball of
paper on the floor by David's chair. Salvador
poked David on the arm and pointed at the ball
of paper. David dutifully dribbled it over to
Salvador's desk with his feet, and Salvador
swooped down to snatch it up.

I kept my eyes on the blackboard, where Mrs.
Bertram had written a note in chalk to remind us
of the extra-credit assignment. The film version
of the book we were reading in class—*Romeo
and Juliet*—was showing at the local movie theater tonight. We had a week to write a one-page
report on it if we wanted the extra credit.

Elizabeth

Unable to resist, I shot a glance at Salvador, but his dark head was bent over his desk.

Was I too harsh? I wondered.

No!

Salvador should never have kissed Anna.

He was a jerk. The jerkiest kind of jerk. A lying, cheating jerk.

All of a sudden another square of paper landed in my lap. I unfolded it and placed it on top of my notebook to read.

Dear Elizabeth,

You're right. Anna does deserve better. And forget about going out with me. You deserve better too. You don't even have to talk to me. But there's one thing I ask: When we're around Anna, promise for now to <u>pretend</u> to be my friend? Because if you totally ignore me, Anna will suspect something, and then we'll both be in deep trouble. And she'll be all alone.

So will you promise? For Anna? Thanks.

Love,
Salvador

p.s. Do you want to go to the extra-credit movie? I'm going to ask Anna.

I didn't write back. As much as I hated to admit it, I knew Salvador was right.

I would have to eat lunch with him and Anna and laugh at Salvador's jokes. I would have to go to *Zone* meetings and pretend that everything was hunky-dory. I might even have to go to the movies with them. And then I would have to listen to Anna gush on the phone tonight about how adorable Salvador was.

I would have to go on lying to Anna just like he was lying to Anna.

For *her* sake.

Bethel

"Bethel! What's wrong?" Jessica asked for the third time.

I was lying on my back on the gritty track, feeling totally humiliated as I looked at her. I ignored the hand she held out to me, got to my feet, and brushed the dust from my running shorts. I had just done something I almost never do.

I'd tripped while running and taken a nasty fall.

I ignored the pain in my knee, but the humiliation was a little harder to overcome. I snatched my water bottle out of Jessica's hand. "Nothing's wrong—I just skinned my knee," I said, although I knew that wasn't what she was talking about.

Jessica smiled and put her hands on her hips. "Bethel, I beat you twice today in warm-up runs, and I'm not even wearing my lucky green shorts because Elizabeth stole them. Something's *got* to be wrong."

She was right. Jessica's a very good runner and getting better every day. But I'm the best runner on the cross-country track team. I'm not bragging.

It's just true. Running is my favorite thing in the whole wide world, and I work hard at it; I never miss a practice. I'm a serious athlete.

So why was my game off?

I tilted back my head and took a long drink from my water bottle, sneaking a glance at the stands that rose alongside the track.

There she was. My sister, Renee. But she was so busy chatting with Coach Krebs that she hadn't even noticed my spill.

I didn't know whether to feel glad that she hadn't seen me fall—or bad that she was paying so little attention to my running.

Jessica shaded her blue-green eyes and followed my gaze to the stands. "Hey—is that your sister up there?" she asked, surprised.

"Um-hmm." I nodded, trying to act like it was no big deal.

"Wow, she looks a lot like you." Jessica smiled and turned back to me. "What's she doing home from college?"

I shrugged. "Who knows? She's probably so perfect, they don't even make her go to class. . . ."

Jessica's eyebrows shot up. She was new this year, and we had only recently become friends after a pretty rocky start. I hadn't told her much about my sister: Renee McCoy, legendary student and track star.

My sister went to Brown University on a scholarship. A *running* scholarship. But she was also a total brain. A smart athlete—what more could you ask for?

It hadn't been easy running in her footsteps. Everywhere I went, I was Renee's little sister.

I'm not Renee's anything! I always felt like shouting. *I'm just me!*

But it wouldn't make any difference. When you had an older sister, people always measured you against her. From kindergarten until now, all my teachers and even some of my friends' parents were always speaking fondly and dreamily of my perfect older sister, Renee. Maybe when I got to high school, I should try to be an exchange student—in Australia!

I frowned up at the bleachers. Renee was doing her usual "charm-the-grown-ups" act. Whatever she was saying, Coach Krebs thought it was hilarious.

"So, was she any good?" Jessica asked.

"Hmmm?"

"At running."

"Oh yeah," I said. "That's how she got to college."

"What, she ran?" Jessica joked.

I had to laugh. "Sort of. She won a full athletic scholarship. Although if that hadn't happened, I'm sure she would have gotten some academic scholarship to pay for everything."

"So is that why you got into track?" Jessica asked me. "'Cause your big sister did it? That's sweet."

"No, it's not!" I growled. I didn't mean to sound so harsh, but I hated being compared to my sister. "I run in *spite* of her. I'm serious. Do you know how humiliating it is to have your teachers compare you to your sister all the time? Especially when they completely worshiped her?"

Jessica laughed. "Actually, I do. Completely. I mean, imagine how you'd feel if she was in the same grade!"

I smiled. But Jessica and her twin seemed like they were really close friends. It was never that way with Renee and me.

Coach Krebs and Renee were looking at me now. Renee made a comment—and then they both laughed.

"Great . . . ," I muttered. "Maybe they did see my fall."

"Don't worry about it. I'm sure your sister used to fall sometimes too," Jessica said. "Anyway, you must be psyched she's home."

"Huh?" I looked at her.

And then I realized—*Jessica didn't get it*.

This wasn't harmless sibling rivalry, like she had with Elizabeth.

I *hated* Renee.

But there was no way I could make Jessica understand.

Forget Renee. Just think about running . . ., I thought.

At least the last part of our practice was cross-country.

I jerked my thumb toward the trail leading into the trees outside the track. "Come on—I'm outta here!" I called, turning to sprint toward the trail. I focused on the trees on the horizon, on my breathing, trying to ignore my sister's eyes boring into my back. . . .

Thunk!

I tripped over a gym bag somebody had left on the ground.

Maybe, I thought with a grimace, *if I lie here long enough, the earth will open up and swallow me whole.*

Instant Messages between Brian Rainey, Kristin Seltzer, and Lacey Frells

BRainE:	Hey you
KGrl99:	How come you didn't call me last nite?
BRainE:	Was I supposed to?
KGrl99:	No. I just thought . . .
BRainE:	I had to go swimming with my little sisters
KGrl99:	Was it fun?
BRainE:	I'd rather have
L88er:	Hey Kristin. What r u doin 2nite?
BRainE:	hung out with you
KGrl99:	Hi Lacey. I'm talking to Brian
L88er:	I thought we could
BRainE:	Kristin?
L88er:	go skating
KGrl99:	I would have liked to hang out with you too
L88er:	I thought you were free
BRainE:	Hi Lacey
L88er:	So u r not free?

KGrl99:	No. I meant yesterday. With Brian
BRainE:	I told you. I went swimming
L88er:	But what about 2nite?
KGrl99:	I know you did
L88er:	What?
BRainE:	What?
KGrl99:	This is too hard. I'm getting off. Bye
BRainE:	Bye. I'll call u
L88er:	Bye Kristin. I'll call u 2
L88er:	Hi Brian.
L88er:	Brian?

A n n a

"Is that you, Anna?" my mother called from the kitchen as soon as I walked in the door that afternoon.

Since when did Mom even notice when I came home from school? I wondered.

"Did you have a nice day?" she asked, coming into the living room.

Stranger still, she was dressed. Not an odd thing for most adults at four in the afternoon. But I'd gotten pretty used to seeing my mom in her bathrobe.

"Look what I got for you today," she said. She pulled something out of a white shopping bag and held it up. It was a dress. A *dress!* I hardly *ever* wear dresses, and when I do, I am *very* picky about what they look like.

This dress was *horrible*—and that's being kind. It looked like something Little Bo Peep would wear.

"Your father kept going on this morning about how I need to get out of the house. So I went

29

shopping." Mom held up the dress in front of me. "I didn't feel like trying anything on. But . . ." She smiled at me. "When I saw this, I just knew I *had* to have it for my little girl."

I hated it when she called me her "little girl." It made me feel like a first-grader.

"Mom, you know I don't wear dresses very much," I said carefully. I didn't want to start anything.

"I know," she said, and put the dress back into the bag. She handed it to me. "But just try it on. Every girl needs a pretty dress. Just in case."

In case what? I wondered. But I didn't say anything. If she wanted to waste money on a dress for me, I couldn't stop her. But she couldn't make me wear it, that's for sure.

Strange. Just when I had started getting used to my mom missing in action all the time, she suddenly turns into Mrs. Brady.

If she gets her hair cut in that little seventies do, I'm out of here! I thought.

I went into the kitchen, dropped my backpack and the shopping bag on the floor, and dumped the mail I had brought in onto the kitchen table. I'd become the official mail sorter in the family—tossing junk mail, stacking bills into a pile for Dad, putting the magazines on the coffee table in the living room. If I left it for Mom, she'd just let it pile up for days.

Mom followed me into the kitchen like a puppy with nothing to do. She began to putter around the counter.

I just shook my head and went through the mail. Junk mail, bill . . . a magazine nobody was going to read . . . bill . . . nothing for me . . . nothing . . .

Wait!

A letter from Lake Tahoe, California, addressed to me! "Yes!" I exclaimed, and ripped it open.

I glanced through the brochure. There were weeklong workshops just for teens on poetry, short-story writing, keeping a journal, even children's books. It was a very popular program, and you had to be recommended by your English teacher. I couldn't wait to go!

"Look, Mom. Isn't this great? And my English teacher is *really* encouraging me to go. She says she'll write my recommendation."

I handed my mom the brochure, and she glanced over it, frowning. "Oh, Anna, it's so far away!" She shook her head. "I don't think we could do without you for a whole week. I'd be so worried."

"What?" I stared at her in disbelief. I'd been to summer sleep-away camps before, and those were *six* weeks long. What was her problem?

Then she just casually opened the cabinet

under the sink and tossed the brochure in the trash! Right in front of me, as if that was that.

I was seething. *She has no right to tell me what I can and cannot do,* I thought, furious. My mother had been absent from my life for a whole year, and I'd taken care of myself pretty well. *How dare she just decide to step in and interfere?*

I walked over to the wastebasket and rescued the brochure. *I'll talk to Dad about it when I see him,* I thought. *If I ever see him.* My dad had been working a lot, leaving early and coming home late. For the past year it seemed like he was never home at all.

"I gotta go do homework," I said, glaring at my mother. I picked up my backpack and headed out of the room.

"Don't forget your dress!" Mom bustled over and handed me the shopping bag.

I snatched the bag out of her hand and hurried upstairs to my room.

I could hear the phone ringing as I closed the door. I closed the blinds too, so my room was as dark as my mood.

Doesn't she know that keeping me home won't keep me safe? I wondered. A tree could fall on me in the backyard. I could get electrocuted spilling soda on my computer. I could slip in the shower and crack my head open.

I sat down at my computer and clicked it on. I put on my headphones and turned the music up loud. I wanted to block out the whole world.

At last I clicked open my poetry file. I was just starting to get in the mood to write when I felt somebody pull up one side of my headphones.

"Knock, knock!" Mom called cheerfully.

I turned and pulled the headphones down around my neck. Mom was standing there, holding a tray. "I thought you could use something nutritious to help you study."

I can't remember the last time my mom made me an after-school snack. And this went way beyond cookies and milk. It was a tray full of hors d'oeuvres!

I wasn't really hungry, but I stuffed a cheese-covered cracker into my mouth. Then I turned back to my computer, hoping my mom would take the hint. Instead she crossed to the window and opened the blinds.

"You need more light," she said. "You'll hurt your eyes."

"I have plenty of light, Mom." I waited for her to leave. But she didn't. She just sort of hovered.

"Who was on the phone?" I asked.

"Salvador," she said. "But I told him you were busy studying—to call back later."

"But Mom—" I couldn't believe it. Since when

did she screen my calls for me? "We're supposed to go to a movie tonight."

"On a school night?"

"It's extra credit for English class," I said. "I told Dad about it this morning. Did Salvador say when he'd be here?"

Mom just pursed her lips. "You need to keep your mind on serious things," she said, smoothing out an invisible wrinkle on my bedspread.

Uh-oh. I hadn't really talked to my mom about how my relationship with Salvador had changed. I hadn't really talked to her about *anything* since Tim died. But had she guessed? Was I that obvious?

It felt really weird for my mother to suddenly try to be so . . . so *involved* with me. *Should I tell her about Salvador?* I wondered.

"Anna," my mother said.

I turned in my chair. She was sitting on my bed now, looking at me. Her expression—I can't describe it. But it gave me the creeps. "What?"

She looked away, and her gaze fell on the framed photograph of Tim. I heard a catch in her throat. "It's been so . . . hard. . . ."

My mom looked so sad. "I know," I whispered. Suddenly I felt really rotten for letting myself get so irritated with her.

Her eyes flicked back at me—she looked so

mournful. I wished I could say something to make her feel better. "Your father and I . . . ," she went on, "we've been talking about you going to see someone."

I frowned at her, puzzled. *See who?*

"To talk," she explained.

"Like . . . like a shrink?" I gasped.

"No!" she exclaimed, rising from the bed. "Nothing like that. Just a . . . counselor. You know. Just someone to talk things over with. Someone . . . who knows . . ." She shrugged helplessly. "Someone who knows what to say. . . ."

"But, Mom!"

"We think it will really do you some good to talk—"

"How could you!" I shouted. I couldn't help it. I was furious. If I wanted someone to talk to, I'd talk to someone I knew—Salvador or Elizabeth—not some *stranger*. No way was I going to tell some weirdo everything I was thinking and feeling. No way—I couldn't.

"But Anna, you need to talk to someone—"

"What if I don't want to!" I yelled. "What if it's nobody's stupid business!"

My mother tried to put her arms around me, but I pulled away. "Anna, listen to me—"

"*You're* the one who needs to talk to someone!" I shouted, out of control. "Not me." I jumped up from my chair and glared at her. "*You're* the one who's messed up and needs help!"

My mother's face paled, and her hand flew to her mouth.

I had never spoken to my mother that way in my whole life. I'd never shouted at her. But the anger inside me was boiling over. It was like I was begging her to argue with me. To yell back at me . . .

But instead she just bowed her head and left the room.

She was hurt. *Well, so am I,* I thought angrily as I flopped onto my bed.

I hadn't realized it, but I guess I had gotten kind of used to my mom being off in her own world. Not bothering me. Never asking questions or poking at my innermost thoughts. Sure, I had missed having her arms to run to, to hold me while I cried.

But I'd been without that for a year.

And now . . . maybe I wanted her to stay out.

Out of my room. Out of my thoughts. Out of my life.

Jessica

"I have to slow down!" I gasped before dropping back on the trail behind Bethel. I was still keeping a pretty good pace, but Bethel surged ahead. My thighs were throbbing as I concentrated on my breathing, desperately trying to avoid getting a cramp in my side. Once I got one, it took hours to get rid of it.

There was no way I could keep up with Bethel today. She was running faster than I'd ever seen her go in practice. Not that she doesn't always run fast. Being on the same team with her had really improved my running—she was the person I chased.

Usually Bethel ran with style and this really cool positive energy, like somebody *born* to run. But not today. Today she didn't look like she was running *toward* the finish line. She looked like she was running *away* from something.

Who, me?

Not likely.

I broke out of the woods and into the field on

the far side of the track behind the bleachers. The afternoon sun blazed in my eyes as I sprinted across the grass to where Bethel was waiting. She was bent over, her legs in a wide lunge, stretching her calves.

I collapsed in the grass next to her, too hot and exhausted to stretch.

"Nice," Bethel commented. "Come on. Let's get showered before you get too comfortable."

She pulled me up, and we headed for the locker room.

"Bethel!" I heard somebody call out. "Wait up!"

But Bethel kept walking, like she hadn't even heard.

"Hey, Bethelina!"

Bethel winced, but she kept on walking. I turned around and looked. It was Renee, walking toward us with a big grin on her face. *Why is Bethel just totally ignoring her?* I wondered.

Then Renee sprinted up to us and grabbed Bethel by the arm. "Hey, sis, are you going deaf or what?" She really did look so much like Bethel—it was weird.

"Hi, Renee." Bethel looked up at her sister. "What are you doing home from school?"

Renee smiled. "Just home for a quick break. Thought I'd come check out your running. So they let you on the team, huh?"

Bethel frowned. "Do Mom and Dad know you're home?"

"Sure." She nodded at me. "Where are your manners, Bethelina? Who's your friend?"

I'd never heard anyone call Bethel "Bethelina" before. It was kind of cute.

"Hi, I'm Jessica Wakefield." I put out my hand, and Renee shook it.

"Nice to meet you," she said. "You look pretty good out there, Wakefield. You sure can run."

"Thanks," I said, flattered by her compliment.

Bethel turned toward the gym door.

"Where are you going?" Renee asked.

"I need a shower," Bethel said. "In case you haven't noticed."

"Oh, I noticed!" Renee joked.

Bethel didn't laugh. She pushed open the door.

"Hey," Renee said to me. "Does everybody still go to Vito's?"

"Yeah," I answered. Vito's Pizza was about the most popular hangout around.

"Great!" Renee said. "Why don't you guys get changed and I'll take you out for pizza? My treat." She looked at me. "You too, Jessica."

"I don't think so . . . ," Bethel started.

"Oh, come on, Bethelina, I insist," Renee said. "What about you, Jessica? Can you come?"

I wasn't really hungry, but behind Renee's

back Bethel was nodding, her eyes wide. I figured she *really* wanted me to go.

"Sure," I said. "Why not?"

"Great!" Renee said. "I'll go get the car and meet you guys out front."

When we got to Vito's, Bethel slid into a booth opposite her sister, so I sat down next to Bethel.

Just then Ethel headed over to our table. She's Vito's wife, about a million years old, and usually pretty grumpy. But not today.

When she spotted Renee, her face lit up in this huge smile—I couldn't believe it. Bethel and I looked at each other as if to ask, "Are we in the right place?"

"Renee McCoy! How are you!" Ethel threw up her big, chubby arms and actually gave Renee a hug.

"I'm great, Ethel," Renee said. "How are you doing?"

"Ah!" Ethel threw her hands in the air. "Busy, busy, busy."

Renee grinned and nodded like she knew exactly what Ethel meant. "You know, Ethel, I haven't had a decent slice of pizza since I went to college." She leaned closer and whispered, "All those *chains!*" She said it like it was a dirty word.

"Ah! That's not pizza!" Ethel said. She whipped her order pad out of her soiled apron and held a pencil over it. "Whaddaya want, my little Renee? For you—it's on the house."

"No, I couldn't—"

But Ethel waved her off. "How often do I get a smart girl like you in here, eh? Now tell me, you want the works?"

Renee looked at Bethel, and she nodded. Then she looked at me.

"Except anchovies, maybe?" I ventured.

Renee grinned. "Everything but anchovies."

"You got it!" Ethel said happily. She eyeballed Bethel in her usual menacing style. "You got a nice big sister there," she said. "You do like her and stay out of trouble, you'll go far."

Bethel jabbed me in the ribs and gave me a "What-did-I-tell-you?" look as Ethel waddled off.

"So, Bethelina," Renee said with a grin. "What's up?"

"Nothing," Bethel said. "And don't call me Bethelina!"

"Oh, come on," Renee said. "I always call you that. You used to like it."

"No, I didn't," Bethel replied, not smiling.

"Sure, you did," Renee said affectionately. She turned to me. "We all used to call her 'Bethelina' and 'Bethelanita.' She was the cutest little kid. She used to sit out in the yard and eat the dirt in our dad's garden. She got so into it, she'd have

41

dirt in her hair and even her underwear!"

I looked at Bethel and started to giggle, imagining her as a quirky little girl who ate dirt.

But Bethel's face looked stony. I guess she was kind of embarrassed.

Renee raised her eyebrows. "So, if you're so grown up now, how come you were eating the track today?"

I couldn't help it—a snort of a laugh burst out of me. It wasn't funny that Bethel fell in practice. It was just funny the way Renee said it.

Bethel glared at me.

"I'm only teasing." Renee laughed. "Don't worry about it. I fall all the time—it's part of running."

I thought that was a nice thing to say. But Bethel just glowered and started fiddling with the saltshaker.

Our pizza arrived faster than I've ever seen it at Vito's.

"Enjoy!" Ethel sang out, smiling at Renee. Then she frowned as her eyes fell on some kids a few booths over. "Eh! Get the dirty sneakers off the seat!" she said, hustling over. "Do you do that at home?"

Renee and I laughed, but Bethel didn't join in.

As we dug into our pizza, Renee told us all about Brown and how cool a university it was. "I love my classes. The track team rules—they call me the Real McCoy! And it's so beautiful in the fall with the leaves changing. . . . You really should think about going there," she told Bethel enthusiastically.

"It sounds awesome," I said. I took a big bite of cheesy pizza.

Bethel shrugged. "Maybe I want to go somewhere else."

"Well, I know it sounds boring since Dad went there and now I'm going there. But you really should check it out. It's just the best."

"Excuse me." Bethel gave me a little shove, and I slid out of the booth for her so she could get up. "I need a refill."

I looked at her cup. It was half full. "But your cup is—"

She glared at me, and I shut up. Whatever. I watched her stride toward the counter. *What is her problem?* I wondered.

"So, how do you like track?" Renee asked me.

"Oh, it's great," I said. "I've never really been into sports much before. Except I used to be a cheerleader at my old school."

Renee wiped her mouth with a napkin. "I'm surprised. You look like you've been running for years."

"Really?" I asked, surprised and flattered at the same time.

Renee nodded. "I'm not kidding. Believe me, I wouldn't say it if I didn't mean it. You have a good, easy stride. And you run like you mean it."

Wow, I thought. *What a nice way to put it: "You run like you mean it."* I couldn't help but smile.

Renee began to tell me a funny story about when she was on the track team at SVJH and Miss Scarlett was coach. Miss Scarlett was our gym teacher, and she was really into personal hygiene.

". . . so Miss Scarlett goes, 'Everyone lift up their arms and smell each other's armpits.' It was a really hot day, and I wasn't wearing enough deodorant. I was *sooo* embarrassed. . . ."

I was giggling when Bethel came back to the table. She gave me this hard, mean stare, kind of the way she used to look at me when she thought I was best friends with Lacey Frells, a snotty, popular girl who Bethel totally detests.

"What's so funny?" Bethel asked as I got up to let her in.

"Oh, nothing," Renee said, waving her hand. "It's a long story." Then she took another big bite of pizza. "Yum, this is *sooo* delicious. I usually don't eat like this."

"You mean with your mouth full?" Bethel cracked.

"Whaddaya mean?" Renee mumbled, her mouth stuffed with pizza. She swallowed and took a sip of her soda. "There's just way too much fat in this stuff. But it is *sooo* good."

Renee chatted on and on about track at Brown. I listened intently. Who knew? Maybe I could aim for a track scholarship at Brown one day. I know Mom and Dad would be pleased at that. After all, Renee seemed to think I was pretty good.

I smiled and took another bite of pizza. I was having a good time.

I glanced at Bethel and realized something strange.

Bethel definitely *wasn't* having a good time. She wasn't acting like herself. She didn't even look like herself. She usually cracks jokes, and she always has a sharp comment or quick comeback. But she just sat there. Eating and looking down at the table.

At last Renee got up to pay the bill. "You guys just sit and finish your pizza."

"I thought the pizza was on the house— since you're so *won*-derful," Bethel said in a smart-alecky voice.

Renee didn't seem to notice the sarcasm. "Yeah, well, Vito and Ethel work really hard," she said. "I can't let them give away free pizzas." She smiled, then headed up to the counter.

I couldn't believe she was going to insist on paying for something that she could have gotten for free. "Wow, your sister's really nice," I said.

I felt Bethel bristle beside me.

I guess I said the wrong thing.

"Nice! Nice? Like when?" Bethel nearly shouted. "Like when she makes fun of me for falling flat on my face? Like when she calls me stupid baby names? Like when she tried to tell me which college I should go to—just so I can be compared to her for four *more* years?"

"I—I—"

Bethel nearly knocked me to the floor trying to scramble out of the booth.

"Bethel, wait," I said. "You're overreacting."

She threw her napkin down on the table and glared at me.

"You just don't get it, Wakefield," she snapped. And then she headed for the door.

I sat there, confused.

But a little bugged too. Renee *was* nice. She'd treated us to pizza. She'd complimented our running. She'd entertained us with fun stories. *She'd* acted normal while *Bethel* sat there like a spoiled brat. I mean, I know Bethel has her hang-ups about her sister. But she'd been downright rude.

"Where's Bethel?" Renee asked as she came back to the table.

"Uh . . ." *Thanks a lot, Bethel. Leave me here to make up excuses for you,* I thought. What was I supposed to say? *Bethel got mad and ran off because I said you were nice?*

I shook my head. "She, uh—just remembered she forgot her math book at school," I fibbed.

Renee frowned and looked toward the door as she picked up her bag and slung it over her shoulder. "I would have driven her over there. She didn't need to walk."

"Maybe she's going to run," I suggested lamely. "You know, to get in some more practice?"

Renee shook her head and left a couple of bills on the table for a tip—a much nicer tip than we usually left.

"Come on, Wakefield," Renee said, and it felt cool the way she called me by my last name. "I'll give you a ride."

On the ride home Renee was quiet for a few minutes. Then she glanced at me. "You know, Bethel's been acting kind of weird." She said it lightly and kept her eyes on the road as she made a turn. "Is something bothering her?"

I gulped. I couldn't tell her the truth. What was I supposed to say? *Yeah. You, Renee.*

I shrugged. "School's kind of hard this year. Especially with track practice almost every day. And we have a big match coming up." Which was all true.

"I don't know," Renee said. "Combining

schoolwork and practice isn't a new thing for Bethel." She sighed. "I think it's something else." She paused at a stoplight and turned her large brown eyes on me. Her look was no-nonsense and straightforward, just like Bethel's.

I couldn't help but squirm.

"Can you find out?" she asked me. "You know, if there's something else bothering her?" Then her eyelids dropped, and she looked away. "Bethel's a lot like me. She tries to be tough. And sometimes she keeps things bottled up inside, but it's really not good for her."

"I—I'll try," I stuttered, unsure what to say. "But don't worry. I'm sure it's nothing."

Renee pressed the accelerator as the light turned green. "Bethel can be a bit of a loner sometimes. I'm glad to see she's made a good friend like you, Wakefield."

Jeez, I thought. *Not only is Renee cool, but she really cares about Bethel.* How come Bethel couldn't see that?

Elizabetn

I was in the kitchen with my fingers wrapped around the lid of a jar of chunky salsa when Jessica came in.

"I can't open this!" I exclaimed in frustration.

Jessica scowled at me and opened the fridge. A can of Coke dropped out and rolled across the floor.

"Grrr!" Jessica growled, and picked up the can.

I unscrewed the salsa lid with one last burst of strength. The glass jar flew out of my hand just as a shower of Coke rained overhead.

I looked at the salsa jar, its guts sloshed out across the floor. Droplets of Coke dripped from my hair and onto my shoulders.

I glanced up at Jessica, who was slurping Coke off her fingers. She started to laugh.

I burst into tears.

"What's wrong?" Jessica cried.

"This whole day stinks!" I choked out between sobs.

I ripped a paper towel off the roll above the

sink and blew my nose. "I don't know," I said miserably. "I guess it's this whole thing with Salvador and Anna—it's driving me crazy!"

Jessica nodded. "I know the feeling. I sort of had a fight with Bethel."

"Really?" I answered, sniffling. "Want to talk about it?"

Jessica shrugged. "It's no big deal, I guess."

"I wish I could say that," I mumbled. "He's such a jerk!"

"I thought you were going to stop talking to El Salvador for a while," Jessica said. She always calls him that—they haven't ever gotten along very well.

"I am. I mean, I'm not going to talk to him unless I absolutely have to." I wiped my eyes. "He's just so . . . *annoying*. Plus we have a math test tomorrow."

"It's ridiculous," Jessica said, slipping her arm around my shoulders. "With everything we have to deal with, they expect us to do *homework?*"

I pressed my head into her shoulder and laughed. Good old Jessica. We were so different in so many ways. And a lot of the time that was tough. But sometimes it was great. Like now— who else but Jessica could make me laugh when I was feeling so completely, pathetically awful?

"Thanks, Jess," I said, smiling at my twin.

"For what?" she asked and took another sip of Coke.

"This is like the first time I've laughed all day."

Jessica looked amazed. "You mean I actually helped you, Miss Perfectly Calm, Cool, and Collected?" She grinned. "What a revelation!"

"Oh, *stop* it!" I said. "I'm not perfect. And you know it!"

"You're not?" She gasped and reached for the kitchen wall phone. "I'd better call the *Sweet Valley News*! This is a big story!"

"Jessica!" I punched her on the arm.

She laughed, then looked at me strangely. "You know, I thought I was going to have to take desperate measures, like call Kristin and drag her to the mall. But I feel much better."

"Really? How come?" I asked.

"'Cause you can be pretty cool sometimes," Jessica said.

Whatever that means! I thought.

"Come on," she said, flinging a sponge at me. "I'll split the cleanup with you!"

Together we mopped up the horrible mess on the floor and settled on some frozen yogurt bars for a snack.

"Hey, want to go to the movies with me tonight?" I asked as we headed upstairs to change out of our sticky clothes. I knew

Elizabeth

Salvador and Anna were definitely going, but they'd be better off on their own. If I went with Jessica, I wouldn't have to sit with them.

Jessica paused halfway up the stairs and turned around. "Miss Perfect, goofing off on a school night? What about math?"

"But this *is* schoolwork!" I protested.

"Sure, it is!"

"No, really," I explained. "It's *Romeo and Juliet*. We get extra credit in English for going to see the movie, remember?"

"Like you *need* extra credit," Jessica shot back.

That's one major difference between me and Jessica. Schoolwork just isn't important to her. She does everything at the last minute, if she does it at all.

I always work ahead, even if I'm getting A's. You never know what might happen on the next test.

"But Jess, that's one of my secrets," I explained. "*Always* do the extra credit. It's like insurance against any mess-ups during the rest of the quarter. Anyway, you're reading the same book—didn't your teacher tell your class about the movie?"

Jessica blinked. "Uh, I guess I didn't get the handout."

I rolled my eyes. "Jessica, what do you *do* in class?"

"My nails?" she said.

I stared at her in horror.

"Just kidding!" she insisted.

I shook my head. "Listen, you'd better come with me. It sounds like you need all the help you can get."

"Okay, okay, I'll go," Jessica said. "On one condition. That you'll help me with my math later."

"It's a deal," I said.

We shook on it, and Jessica ran up the rest of the stairs to figure out what to wear.

I couldn't help but feel lucky. Sure, my twin drives me absolutely nuts sometimes. But I would much rather be with Jessica than anyone else.

Particularly Salvador.

Or Anna—at least while she's going out with Salvador.

My sister will always be my best friend forever.

Salvador

I had walked up the steps to Anna's house a million times without a thought. Without calling. Just to stop by and hang out.

Weird how one simple, spur-of-the-moment kiss can make your whole life change.

This time I had called ahead. But Anna's mom said she was studying. Her voice sounded odd, sort of mechanical, and she hung up before I could explain that Anna and I had made plans to see that film for English.

Now I felt really awkward standing on the Wangs' front steps, ringing the doorbell. Like I was some kind of stalker or something.

Lighten up, I told myself. *It's just Anna.*

Maybe I was thinking about everything too much. Anna and I had been friends for such a long time. Maybe if I just quit fighting it—*and quit thinking about Elizabeth*—going out with Anna might actually be a great thing.

Anna was pretty. Smart. And I was good friends with her. What more could a guy ask for?

I rang the bell again. *Ding-ding, ding-ding*—

"All right, already!" Anna shouted, flinging open the front door.

I winced. Something told me "the girl of my dreams" was *not* in a good mood.

I heard her mother call something from behind her.

"I don't *need* a jacket!" Anna hollered over her shoulder. Then she sighed loudly, disappeared a second, and came back with a red jacket on.

She slammed the door behind her, ripped off the jacket, and tossed it onto the porch swing.

Whoa! I had never seen her talk back to her mother like that.

Anna skipped up to me and planted a kiss on my cheek. "Hi, Salvador," she chirped, beaming up at me.

What is going on? I wondered. It was like Anna's personality had changed in the space between me and the front door. One minute she was yelling, and the next she was all perky and sweet.

I swallowed and looked down at her. "Anna, are you all right?" I asked. "Do you want to talk about it?"

Anna blinked, like *I* was the one acting strange. "I'm fine," she said, and smiled again.

When I just stood there, staring, with my mouth hanging open, she tugged on my sleeve.

"Come on," she said sweetly. "Let's go."

"Are you sure?" I asked again, studying her dark brown eyes. "Did you and your mom have a fight?"

Anna looked away. "Let's just go," she said, and ran down the steps.

I jumped down the steps and began to walk alongside her. Anna was completely silent. When we reached the corner, I asked her again, "Why won't you tell me what's wrong?"

Anna stopped in her tracks and whirled around.

"Everything!" she exploded. "My mother! She ignores me for a whole year, and now all of sudden she's all over me. It's like she suddenly remembered I'm there."

I frowned. "Well, that's good, isn't it?"

"Good?" Anna exclaimed, shaking her head.

Oops. "I meant bad," I corrected myself.

"It's terrible," Anna replied. "What does she think she's doing? It's like she's fussing over me, fixing me snacks and making me wear a coat so she can make up for not saving Tim."

"That's a little harsh, don't you think?" I said, trying to be reasonable.

Anna's glare told me I'd said the wrong thing again.

In the old days, BK—Before Kiss—I would have tried to tease her out of her bad mood. But today I was second-guessing everything I said.

56

Thinking too much. So I clammed up. I didn't feel like getting yelled at. Especially when I hadn't done anything wrong. Especially when I was doing her such a favor by . . .

By what? I asked myself. *By being her boyfriend?* Man, did that ever sound creepy. Love wasn't supposed to be something you did for charity. I was really in trouble.

I stuffed my hands in my pockets and kept walking. I felt really gloomy. And I'm not a gloomy kind of guy. But at least I was there—I mean, being there for Anna. That's what I was supposed to be doing. And I *was* doing it, wasn't I?

"Anyway," Anna said, forcing a smile and tucking her hand under my arm. "Forget it, Sal. Let's just have *fun.*"

Great, I thought miserably. *Anna's world is falling apart, and I'm supposed to be her happy-go-lucky* boyfriend.

I wasn't feeling very cheerful, but I pressed up the corners of my mouth and glanced down at Anna's sad face. It was a lame attempt at a smile.

At the corner of Arbor Drive and Booker Creek Road, I turned right. Anna's hand had slipped off my arm, and a few steps down the sidewalk I realized I was by myself. I stopped and looked around.

Anna was standing with her hands on her

hips, frowning at me. "Where are you going?" she demanded.

Was this another trick question? "To the movie?" I answered.

"Right. It's that way," Anna said, and pointed down Arbor Drive.

I may not be a genius. But I've lived in that neighborhood for nine years, and I definitely knew the quickest way to the movie theater. "You gotta be kidding me. It's this way," I said.

"But Booker Creek Road is ugly," she said. "Arbor Drive is nicer—it'll be romantic."

Oh no. I stared at her. "But that's so much longer!" I insisted.

"No, it's not," Anna insisted. "It's just a different way. It's better."

I shook my head. "Booker Creek is at least ten minutes faster."

"And faster is always better," she said sarcastically.

"Anna, you know I hate to miss the previews."

"We're not going to miss the previews," she said. She folded her arms. "I want to go on Arbor Drive."

I rolled my eyes. "Come on, Anna. Quit being stubborn. We'll be late for the movie."

Her eyes flashed. "Stubborn?"

I knew I'd made a mistake with that comment. "Sorry, Anna. It's just that—"

"Since you already seem to think I'm a stubborn mule, I will live up to your expectations and go the way I originally wanted," she announced. "See you there."

I watched her walk away. I almost called her bluff and started walking the other way. But I figured that would only get me in more trouble. So I gave in and jogged down the sidewalk till I caught up with her.

We walked the rest of the way in silence.

As we neared the movie theater, I began to slow down. I glanced nervously at Anna.

The movie was for school. But it was sort of a date too.

Was I supposed to pay?

As we got in line, I saw that Anna didn't seem to be reaching for any money.

"Two students, please," I said to the girl behind the glass.

"Since when do you pay for me?" Anna demanded instantly.

"Uh, but I thought—"

"I pay my own way," she said.

The cashier tapped on the window. "Make up your mind," she said. "There are people waiting."

"One, please," Anna said, cutting in front of me and sliding her money in through the tiny mouse-hole opening.

The girl gave Anna her ticket and change. Then I bought my own ticket and we hurried inside. *Did I do something wrong?* I wondered.

The snack bar was crowded since it was almost time for the movie to begin. I waved to David from English and this girl Carla who's in my math class. At last we got to the front of our line.

"We'll have two large buttered popcorns, a large and a medium Coke, and one big pack of Raisinets," I said, ordering what we always got.

"How do you know what I wanted?" Anna demanded.

I stared at her. "But we always get the same thing," I protested. "Like, since we were eight."

"Yeah? Well . . ."

She couldn't argue with that. I smiled, as if to say, "I told you so."

Big mistake.

"Well, maybe I've had so many Raisinets, I'll puke if I have another one!" Anna answered.

"Come on, Anna, you're just being silly."

"First I was stubborn—now I'm silly?" Anna snapped.

When was I ever going to learn to keep my mouth shut?

When the girl came back with my change, Anna said to her, "I'll have one medium popcorn—no butter, a large Sprite, and a box"—she stared pointedly at me— "of Nerds."

The girl left to fill Anna's order.

"Anna! What am I supposed to do with all this?" I demanded, gesturing at all the food stacked in front of me.

Anna shrugged. "You ordered it. You paid for it. You eat it."

Then she gathered up her food and marched into the theater.

What is her problem? I thought. I put my food onto a paper tray so I could carry it all, then tried not to spill anything as I hurried after her. *I know things are bad, but who wants to date someone who yells at you all the time?* Anna was making it kind of hard not to tell her that I really didn't want to go out with her in the first place.

When my eyes had adjusted to the darkening theater, I saw Anna about halfway down the aisle. "Let's sit here," she said when I caught up with her.

"In the middle?" I asked, taken aback. Since when did we *ever* sit in the middle? We always sat down front. It made us feel like we were right *in* the movie.

"Yeah. It's the best spot," Anna insisted.

"But we always sit down front."

"Things change." She shrugged.

"Come on, Anna. How about those two seats in the front row?" I suggested.

"Sit where you like," she said, and scooted over to the middle seat.

I felt like leaving her alone and going down to sit in the front row all by myself. I really did. But I was doing my best to keep her happy, so I followed her. "I just hope nobody sits next to me," I said. "I hate getting boxed in."

We sat down. I put my extra popcorn and sodas down on the floor as the lights went down and those movie notices started playing. No smoking. We love babies, but please take them to the lobby when they cry. Don't be a slob—put your trash in the cans and not on the floor. They're so hokey, they're funny.

I sat back, dug out a fistful of popcorn, and stuffed it in my mouth.

Anna glared at me.

"Wha—?" I said, my mouth full.

"Nothing," she hissed, and looked away.

I finished chewing my popcorn and swallowed, suddenly self-conscious. I'd never thought about how I ate popcorn. Was it disgusting?

Then I glanced at Anna.

I couldn't believe how *she* ate popcorn.

She took one piece of popcorn at a time—no joke. One! And put it in her mouth and chewed.

Weird!

What was even weirder was that I'd never noticed how she ate popcorn before. How could she even taste it?

I shook my head and started eating my own popcorn again. The normal way: by the handful.

"Shhh," Anna said.

"What?" I whispered. "I didn't say anything."

"You're making too much noise," she said. "I can't hear."

I glanced at the screen. Little cartoon popcorn boxes and soda cups with goofy faces were dancing across the screen.

"You want me to be quiet so you can hear the snack-bar commercial?"

"Well, the movie will be on soon," she said. "And you always make too much noise."

"Well, you always talk too much," I shot back.

Her head whipped around. "I do not."

"You do too," I said. "As soon as I start getting into it, you start blabbing." I changed my voice to sound like a girl's. "Like, 'Ooh, isn't that a cute outfit? That's Jenny What's-her-name from *Derek's Falls*.' It totally ruins the movie."

"*I'm* ruining the movie for *you?*" she said incredulously.

"Shhh," I said, glancing around. "Keep your voice down. People are starting to stare."

"I—" She clamped her mouth shut and sank down in her seat. The movie was beginning to start. The titles ran, and the whole cast was listed—the way they always do with old movies—to crackling music.

I was just beginning to concentrate when Anna whispered, "Quit being mean to me."

I realized she must have been stewing since that last comment.

"Well, you're not exactly a joy to be with," I whispered back.

"Hey," somebody cracked behind us, "could you two have your little lovers' quarrel outside?"

Anna froze and remained still, her eyes glued forward. She was embarrassed, I could tell. She's not one to make a scene in public.

"Don't worry about it," I whispered. "Just cool it."

"Cool it? You want me to cool it?" she said. "Fine. I'll cool it." She stood up. "I'll cool the whole stupid thing!" She shoved her popcorn, candy, and drink into my arms. "I don't want to go out with you anymore, Salvador del Valle! In fact, I never want to see you again!"

"Is that a promise?" I shot back.

Once more, I should have kept my mouth shut.

Anna looked so angry, I was afraid her hair was going to burst into flames.

But instead of turning into fire, she turned into ice.

"Excuse me," she said crisply, climbing over my feet. "Excuse me . . . excuse me . . . ," I heard her say as she stumbled over the other people to get to the aisle.

I warned her not to sit in the middle.

When she was gone, I sank down into my seat and blew out my breath. I felt horrible. Like a basketball team that had just gotten creamed by its biggest rival. I was angry, I was frustrated, I was embarrassed, I was . . .

Relieved?

Whoa. That was a surprise.

But if I was totally honest, I had to admit I *was* relieved. As if a heavy weight had just been lifted from my shoulders.

I let out a long sigh and rested my head back against the seat. I didn't have to pretend to be Anna's boyfriend anymore. And I could watch the movie in peace.

Then I felt someone tap me on the shoulder.

She's back! I panicked.

But it wasn't Anna. It was Brian Rainey, climbing over the seat backs to flop into the seat Anna had just evacuated.

"Is this seat taken?" Brian asked.

"Not anymore," I muttered.

"That's what I thought." I could see Brian's grin in the flickering light from the movie screen. "The little scenario going on down here is a lot more interesting than this boring movie, I'll tell you that."

I just shrugged. What could I say?

"You having a party or something?" Brian whispered.

"What?"

He pointed at all the snacks in my lap and on the floor—popcorn, soda, candy.

"Oh," I said. "It's extra. Help yourself."

"All right," Brian said greedily. "Thanks."

I glanced around. "Who'd you come with?" I whispered.

"Nobody."

"Smart move," I muttered.

Brian chuckled softly. "I was supposed to come with Kristin, but Lacey talked her into going skating. I wanted to sit with you guys, but . . ." He shrugged as if he was happy to just let the subject drop.

I shrugged back in reply and slumped down in my seat to watch the movie.

I have to say it was a heck of a lot better being there with Brian than with Anna. Brian didn't talk at all. And he didn't seem to care how I ate my popcorn.

During the whole movie I couldn't stop thinking about Anna.

I'd been Anna's friend a whole lot longer than I'd been her boyfriend, and I cared about her. I didn't want her to feel bad. Or to be mad at me. Even though I was mad at her for snapping at me and relieved that she had broken up with me, I still felt really crummy for snapping back at her.

But not crummy enough to try to get her back (as a girlfriend, I mean).

She'll see, I thought. *She'll see now that it's best that we're just friends.*

Then I remembered Anna's face and how truly angry she'd looked when she left.

If *we're still friends* . . .

Elizabeth

"Whoa—catch the action down there," Jessica whispered to me around a mouthful of popcorn.

Like I could miss it, I thought. "Shhh!" I whispered back, and forced my eyes back up to the screen.

I hadn't been watching anything else since I'd seen Salvador and Anna sit down several rows in front of us. How could I, when a major fight broke out between my newest best friend and my . . . my . . .

What exactly was Salvador to me anyway?
Nothing!

Extra credit, I reminded myself. *Pay attention so you can get the extra credit.*

Then suddenly the action on the screen was interrupted by the silhouette of Anna jumping to her feet.

I couldn't hear her words, but her body language spoke loud and clear. She was upset.

"Hey, down in front!" somebody called out. A couple of guys behind me cracked up.

Anna turned and stared, then stumbled down the aisle.

"Anna!" I whispered loudly as she hurried past my row. But she seemed not to hear me.

"Was she crying?" Jessica asked me.

"I think so!" I handed my popcorn to my sister and hurried up the aisle after Anna.

I blinked in the bright light of the lobby and caught Anna's dark ponytail as she disappeared into the ladies' room.

I pushed in after her.

"Anna?" I called.

The stalls all looked empty, but then I saw Anna's white sneakers beneath the door at the far end. The door wasn't closed, and when I peeked in, I saw that she was leaning up against the wall, crying.

"Anna!" I said gently, touching her elbow. "What's wrong?"

At first she just shook her head, unable to speak. I pulled some toilet paper off the roll and handed it to her. She wiped her eyes and blew her nose.

"I just . . ."—*sniff*—"broke up . . ."—*snort*—"with Sal . . . ," she managed to stammer.

My heartbeat quickened. I immediately felt *glad*. Salvador and Anna weren't a couple anymore! Now I could . . .

What? I asked myself. *Don't be an insensitive jerk like Salvador—comfort Anna!*

69

"What happened?" I asked gently, offering her some more toilet paper.

"Oh, I don't know. It's everything. He can't be my boyfriend. It's all wrong," she cried. "I told him I never wanted to talk to him again!"

Wow. That *was* a big deal. She and Salvador had been friends since they were little kids.

"And then my mom . . ."

Anna stopped, her lower lip trembling. *How dare you, Salvador,* I thought. *How dare you make Anna cry.* She had enough to cry about without him.

"What about your mom?" I asked.

Anna wiped her tears away with the back of her hand. "She's suddenly gone from locking herself in the bedroom to climbing all over me! And she and Dad want me to see a shrink!"

"What?"

"Yeah, to talk about . . ." She stopped, and I thought she was about to burst into tears once more.

Then she hiccuped.

We looked at each other, eyes wide, and burst out giggling. Even though nothing was funny, there was something about that hiccup that sounded hilarious.

"Why are we laughing?" Anna asked, still giggling.

"I don't know!" I giggled back.

Anna took a deep breath and let it out. She walked over to the sink and splashed her face with cold water. "I'm okay," she said, sounding more like her normal self as she dried her face with paper towels. She crushed the towels up into a ball and tossed them in the garbage. Then she crossed her arms, whirling around to face me, her eyes flashing in anger. "Sal is a jerk! A total jerk, isn't he?" she demanded.

It was more like a statement of fact than a question.

I opened my mouth, but nothing came out. Was I allowed to be mad at Salvador now too? Or would that be revealing too much?

But Anna didn't need an answer. She started rehashing everything Salvador had said or done since they first kissed. Actually, not that much had happened. How much *could* happen in only a week?

". . . and then, when I said I never wanted to speak to him again, he said, 'Is that a promise?' I mean, isn't that the *meanest* thing you've ever heard anybody say?"

I nodded. It *was* mean. And I was furious with him for saying it.

Now, I thought. *Now you can say whatever you want about Salvador.* He had proved it—he was as low as they come.

I frowned. "I can't believe he said that!"

Anna looked at her feet. "I thought he was

my friend. I thought he understood. Especially about . . ."

She didn't say about what. But I knew the missing word was *Tim*.

And then all her anger overflowed into tears once more. "I can't handle this right now . . . ," she sobbed.

I couldn't believe it. How could Salvador be so mean to Anna when he knew she was having such a hard time?

She was miserable. And it was all Salvador's fault.

Besides, what was he doing going out with Anna in the first place?

"What a total jerk," I muttered aloud.

"Yeah," Anna agreed, dashing her tears away with the back of her hand. "I know, let's make a pact. That we're never going to speak to Salvador del Valle ever again." She held up the little finger on her right hand, her eyes narrowed. "Pinkie swear?"

"What?" I laughed. I hadn't made a pinkie swear since Jessica and I were in third grade.

"Come on!" Anna insisted, waving her pinkie in the air and sniffling. "Girls have to stick together."

"Yeah," I agreed. "Boys stink. Especially Salvador."

We hooked pinkies.

"I swear I will never, ever talk to Salvador del Valle ever again in my whole life," we said together.

Anna smiled at me like I was her best friend in the whole world.

It should have been a good feeling.

But in my heart I knew I hadn't been totally honest with Anna. I mean, I was mad at Salvador for *completely* different reasons than she was.

At least we were united against a common enemy.

We unlocked pinkies, and I pulled a wad of paper towels out of the dispenser and handed them to Anna.

"Maybe I should just go home," Anna said when she had blown her nose for the last time.

"Don't," I said. "Come back in and watch the movie. You can sit with me and Jessica. It'll take your mind off everything. And don't forget—it's extra credit."

Extra credit is a powerful draw. Or maybe Anna just didn't want to be alone.

"All right," she agreed. "But be really quiet so Salvador doesn't turn around. And the minute it's over, we have to run out—he always stays until the music stops anyway."

"Okay," I agreed. "Don't worry."

As we snuck back into our seats, I glanced at Salvador's seat. Someone was sitting with him—it looked like Brian. And Salvador had sunk down into his seat, so I could barely see the top of his dark, curly head.

Good. Maybe Anna can forget about him for now, I thought.

Maybe I can forget about him too.

Instant Messages between Brian Rainey, Kristin Seltzer, and Lacey Frells

Kgrl99:	How was the movie?
BRainE:	Scary
Kgrl99:	Really?
BRainE:	And I'm stuffed. I ate too many Nerds
Kgrl99:	'Cause u are a *nerd!*
BRainE:	Am not
Kgrl99:	Are too
BRainE:	Then why are you talking to me?
Kgrl99:	Nerds can be cute
BRainE:	Is *this* nerd cute?
L88er:	Hey Kristin you skating queen
BRainE:	or at least cuter than most?
L88er:	What are you guys talking about? O my
Kgrl99:	U know it.
L88er:	God Kristin you have to come meet Gel's
BRainE:	Um what's up Lacey?
Kgrl99:	Lacey can I call u later?

L88er:	cousin—he's like *the* biggest
BRainE:	I gotta go help my sis with her art project
L88er:	hottie ever!! Oh hi Brian
Kgrl99:	'Nite Brian
BRainE:	Sleep well
L88er:	Kristin? R u there?

Tuesday Morning

8:09 A.M.   Jessica and Elizabeth arrive at school and step off their bus. Anna is waiting for Elizabeth at the school entrance.

8:11 A.M.   Salvador spots Elizabeth and Anna walking arm in arm down the hallway at school. He opens his locker to hide his face.

8:13 A.M.   On her way to homeroom Jessica sees Bethel talking to Ginger from the track team. She hurries over to join them.

8:13 A.M.   Bethel sees Jessica walking toward her with a friendly smile on her face. Bethel ducks into the ladies' room and leaves Ginger standing there, staring after her.

8:14 A.M.   Jessica follows Bethel into the ladies' room. She begins talking to the pair of feet she believes are Bethel's underneath the stall door. The toilet flushes, the door opens, and a very tall, very cool ninth-grader named Callie sneers down at her. Jessica blushes and looks around for Bethel, but she is nowhere to be seen.

Jessica

I'd been trying all morning to talk to Bethel, but it almost seemed like she was avoiding me.

She couldn't still be mad about the thing with Renee at Vito's, could she?

Between third and fourth period I spotted her at the water fountain near the front office.

"Bethel!" I called out.

You know how it is when you know somebody hears you or knows you're looking at them but pretends they don't?

That's how Bethel was acting.

Well, I wasn't going to let her get away with it.

"Bethel," I called again as I pushed through the crowd. I had almost reached her when suddenly—

She popped into the principal's office directly across from the water fountain.

Fine, I thought. *I don't want to talk to her that badly.*

I shrugged and walked on to my next class, wondering what Bethel was going to dream up

78

to say to the principal's secretary about why she was in his office.

By lunchtime I decided I was going to corner her and *make* her talk to me. I saw her sitting at a table all alone, her back to me.

I slapped my tray down directly across from her and sat down. She immediately stood up, as if to leave.

"If you leave without letting me talk to you, I'll scream," I warned.

Bethel stared at me like I was nuts. She knew me well enough to know that I actually might scream.

"Come on," I said. "Sit down. Talk to me. Please?"

Bethel sat down and put her napkin in her lap. Then she opened her milk carton and stuck in a straw. She took a bite of tossed salad.

So she was staying, but not talking.

"Hel-*lo,*" I said. "It's me—Jessica."

She pulled *Romeo and Juliet* out of her back-pack and started reading it.

It was a pretty good book—at least the movie was cool and creepy—but it wasn't *that* good.

"Come on, Bethel," I said in exasperation. "What did I do? So what if I talked to your sister? It's called good manners. *You're* my friend, not her."

Bethel shrugged and put down her book. I was making progress.

"Anyway, I know how you feel," I said more gently.

"No, Jessica. You don't know how I feel," Bethel said. Her lower lip trembled, and all at once the words came tumbling out. "It's *horrible* being Renee's sister. She's always been better. The smartest one. The one who wins trophies and scholarships and awards. At family reunions all the grown-ups talk to her like she's one of them and I get stuck with the babies. It's like I'm *invisible*."

"Oh, Bethel, I'm sorry," I said.

"You'd think since she's so much older than me that it wouldn't matter at school," Bethel went on. "But it always has. Her teachers always remember her, and they're always comparing us. And my parents are the worst. When I wanted to take chorus, they were like, 'But *Renee* took band.' Or, '*Renee* never got a B in math.' Or, 'Remember when *Renee* won that award for blah blah blah. . . .'"

I put my hand on Bethel's arm. "I know. I totally understand."

"No, you don't—"

"I *do!*" I nearly shouted in my impatience. "Try being Miss Perfect's *twin!*"

Bethel's eyes widened. "Yeah," she said at last. "But you're *friends* with your sister. I'm not—I hate my sister."

"But Renee's off at college most of the time," I said, frustrated. "Maybe if you kind of forgot about her, everybody else would too."

"How can I forget about her when everyone keeps reminding me?" Bethel said, pounding her tray with her fist. A few kids at the next table turned to stare at her and then went back to their lunch.

Bethel leaned toward me and lowered her voice. "She's always in my face, every second of every day. In the trophies on the shelf in the living room. In everything my parents and my teachers say, always measuring everything I do against some perfect standard set by Renee." She poked angrily at her salad. "And Renee *knows* she's the favorite."

"Oh, Bethel, she is not the favorite," I said. "My mom always says it's impossible for a mother to love one kid more than another. Besides, Renee is worried about you. She doesn't understand why you're so angry with her all the time."

Bethel's eyes blazed. "How do you know what my sister thinks?" she demanded.

"Well . . . yesterday, when you left, she gave me a ride home," I said. "And she asked me some questions. Like if you were mad, or was something bothering you. I said—"

"Oh! So you two were talking about me behind

81

my back?" she exclaimed. "That's just great."

"It wasn't like that," I insisted. "She wanted—"

"I don't care what she wanted," Bethel shot back. "Haven't you heard a word I said?" She shoved her lunch tray across the table and leaped from her chair.

"Bethel, wait—"

But Bethel didn't even glance back as she strode out of the cafeteria.

It felt pretty terrible eating lunch alone after that conversation. I got out my math book and pretended to study for my test that afternoon while I ate. But I was too mad at Bethel to concentrate.

I was only trying to help her.

It's not my fault she doesn't like her sister, I thought bitterly.

And Bethel wasn't the only kid in the world who'd ever been compared to an older sister. Elizabeth, of course, had stayed up late last night after the movie, studying for math. She'd offered to study with me, but I didn't feel like it. I just read a magazine until I fell asleep.

She was only a few minutes older, but she was definitely the model child.

The bell rang. I closed my math book and put it in my backpack. I was probably going to be way too busy feeling inferior to *my* older sister after my math test to worry much about my fight with Bethel.

82

ZONE'S
MINUTE MOVIE REVIEWS

BECAUSE WHO WANTS TO READ A LONG, BORING REVIEW?

BY BRIAN RAINEY AND SALVADOR DEL VALLE

Brian

Let's face it. I would never have gone to see *Romeo and Juliet* except for extra credit in English class.

But I was surprised. I thought it was going to be a sappy love story with boring dialogue, but after a while I got seriously into the story. It's really cool.

There was a lot of action and intrigue and some really good fight scenes.

And the acting is great, too.

I don't want to spoil it for you, but the ending totally blew me away.

If you like cool movies, do yourself a favor and go see it. You'll like it.

If you hurry, you might still score the extra credit!

RATING: ****

Salvador

It was a boring love story.

RATING: 4 GROANS.

(And the popcorn was too salty.)

A n n a

Dear Diary,
  I don't know what I'd do
without Elizabeth. I was so
nervous about bumping into
Salvador at school, but
Elizabeth went everywhere
with me. She even brought
an extra sandwich in her
lunch and we ate outside on
the steps, just in case
Salvador was waiting for
us—like the stupid jerk that
he is—at our usual table.
  It feels good to be mad at
him. Elizabeth and I wrote
his name in her notebook
and then scribbled over it,
hard, until the paper
started to rip!

I thought since Salvador and I had been such good friends for so long that he would just know how to make me feel better and that he would be the best boyfriend I could have. I know I wasn't being completely fair. He didn't. He wasn't. I was, wrong. But that doesn't mean he had to be a complete jerk about it and say mean things to me. I mean, I never did anything to him.

Elizabeth and I are still going to the <u>Zone</u> meeting, but we're not going to talk to Salvador. If we have anything to say, we'll tell Brian, and he can tell Salvador if he wants to.

Elizabeth

"Hey, Lizzie," Jessica called, and pulled me over to her locker. "You look terrible—are you okay?"

I was in a bad mood. Leave it to my sister to make me feel even worse.

I tucked my hair behind my ears and looked down at my gray twinset and black jeans. I thought I looked pretty good, actually.

"No." Jessica shook her head, laughing at me. "Your *face*. You're all like this—" She scrunched up her eyes and her mouth. She looked like a shrunken apple.

"Thanks," I said. But I knew what she meant. I'd been palling around all morning with Anna and avoiding Salvador. I had a math test next period. I was having the worst day of my life.

"I'm kind of stressed out, I guess."

"Tell me about it." Jessica rolled her eyes. "We have that math test that *someone* did not help me study for *at all*. And Bethel's still totally not talking to me."

"Why don't you write her a note?" I suggested.

Salvador and I had managed to communicate our feelings pretty well through notes. Not that it had gotten us anywhere.

"Hey, thanks," Jessica said. "That's a great idea."

"And don't worry about math, Jess. You'll do okay."

I know it's mean—I love my sister. But I really wanted to be alone. "Look," I pointed out. "There's Damon Ross talking to Kristin."

Jessica didn't even pause. She's had the biggest crush on Damon ever since school started, and Kristin is her friend. I knew she wouldn't miss an opportunity like that. She zoomed down the hallway without looking back.

Now at least I can walk to class in peace, I thought. I hitched my backpack up on my shoulder and headed down the hall, stopping to grab a drink at the water fountain.

I bent my head and closed my eyes as I swallowed the painfully cold water.

"Elizabeth," somebody whispered urgently in my ear.

My eyes flew open, and I lifted my head with a start.

Anna was standing right next to me.

"Shhh," she said, holding her index finger to her lips. She was watching something behind me, her face tense and wary. Then she relaxed. "It's okay. He's gone."

I wiped my mouth. "Who?" I asked.

"Salvador. He was right behind you. It looked like he was going to come over, but then he turned around when he saw me."

"Oh," I said, feeling uncomfortable.

Our pinkie swear was less than a day old, but I was already getting kind of tired of it. I mean, how long could we go on like this? Anna and Salvador had known each other too long to just completely stop talking to each other. And I hated being caught in the middle.

There had to be another way. But so far I hadn't thought of anything.

"Anyway, I have to go to Spanish," Anna said. "I'll meet you at your locker right before the *Zone* meeting, okay?"

"Okay," I agreed. "See you later, Anna."

"Good luck with math," she called, and turned to leave.

I have to say, I was glad to see her go.

It was almost easier to have no friends at all than friends you didn't talk to or friends who you couldn't tell the whole truth to.

And I was a lousy friend anyway.

Dear Bethel,

I know you don't want to talk to me, and that's okay. But I really wish you would because I could explain everything, and then maybe you wouldn't be mad at me anymore.

Your sister asked me if you were okay because she thought you'd been acting weird. Which you kind of were. But I couldn't say that it was because of her. That would have been really mean. So I just told her I'd try and find out what was wrong. But it's not like I'm spying on you for her or anything. I mean, she didn't ask me to do that. She was just looking out for you.

I know you don't want advice, but since you're already not talking to me, I have nothing to lose. I think you should talk to your sister and tell her what's bothering you. See, that's why things never get too bad between me and my sister. Sometimes we scream and yell, but we always end up talking about it

and make up. Anyway, Renee has no
idea how you feel. So maybe you
should tell her.

That's all I have to say.

I hope you decide to talk to me
again because I miss you.

Love,

Jessica

A n n a

We have **Zone** meetings wherever we can have access to a computer. Today it was in the language lab.

Seeing Salvador was the last thing Elizabeth and I wanted to do. But *Zone* was important to us. We had to be there.

When we walked in, one side of the room was filled with people wearing headphones and mouthing words in French and Spanish. Salvador and Brian were already sitting at a little table on the other side of the room, with their backs to us.

I nudged Elizabeth's arm, and we started to walk toward them. I kept my gaze just above their heads.

Just ignore him, I told myself. *Just pull up a chair and get to work.*

Salvador and Brian were deep in conversation.

"You must have the kiss of death," I heard Brian say as we came up. "Every girl you make out with ends up mad at you. If you don't stop hooking up with our staff, we won't be able to put out the magazine."

I snapped to attention. Were they talking about me? What did he mean, "every girl"? Who else had Salvador kissed?

"What," I said loudly, walking around to face them, "do you mean by that?"

Brian sat bolt upright as if I'd caught him stealing from his grandmother. He glanced nervously at Salvador.

Salvador swallowed and stared at Elizabeth.

I looked at her for support, but a pink blush had washed over her face.

What did she have to blush about? *I'm the one who should be embarrassed.*

"Salvador's bragging about one stupid kiss," I said. "Big deal."

Elizabeth's blush deepened to a blazing red.

I stared at her, confused. But she was looking at the floor.

Nobody said anything.

"Elizabeth?" I asked again.

She glanced up at me, and those blue-green eyes told me everything. Like I was reading her thoughts without even trying.

And at that moment, I knew.

For a few seconds my heart stopped beating. I could feel the blood rushing to my head.

"Wait a minute—you and Salvador?" I glanced at Salvador, waiting for him to deny it.

But all he did was squirm and look away.

"Way to go, Brian," he muttered.

So it was true. Salvador *had* kissed Elizabeth.

I felt like I was going to throw up. I was so totally, completely humiliated.

My mind raced.

Salvador and Elizabeth hadn't known each other that long. When had they had time to kiss?

"When?" I demanded when I found breath enough to speak. "Where?"

No one said anything.

And Salvador and I had been going out for a week. Had he kissed Elizabeth *recently?* Had he cheated on me?

"Why?" I asked angrily.

"Anna . . ." Elizabeth reached out her hand to me, a miserable, guilty look in her eyes.

But I backed away from her. I didn't want her to touch me. I didn't care how bad she felt. Just like she and Salvador obviously didn't care how *I* felt.

When were they alone together? I wondered again.

I racked my brain, searching for a time when they could have snuck a kiss. And then I knew. The party at the Wakefields', when those high-school guys started drinking . . . I had looked everywhere for Elizabeth to tell her what was going on. I couldn't find her. . . .

Anna

Those stupid drunk guys got me so upset. I wanted to talk to Salvador.

But Salvador and Elizabeth had been off kissing somewhere.

Traitors.

I couldn't believe it. Here I'd been trying to get Elizabeth to gang up on Salvador, spilling my guts out to her. And all that time she and Sal had been secretly kissing. It was unbelievable.

"How could you!" I shouted at Salvador.

"Anna—," he started.

But I didn't want to listen.

"And you," I said to Elizabeth, fighting back tears. "You lied to me! That's so low!"

I whirled back to Salvador. "What was I? Some kind of booby-prize girlfriend? How could you kiss *me* when you were thinking of *her*?"

"Anna," Salvador said, standing up. "I never meant that to happen—"

"Oh," I said. "So you just kissed me like I was some kind of charity case!"

"No," Salvador insisted. "It wasn't like that."

"Like I'm going to believe anything *you* have to say," I snapped.

"Hey, Anna," Brian interrupted. "I'm sorry I said what I did. I didn't mean—"

"You're a bigmouthed idiot!" I yelled, totally out of control now. "Thanks for ruining my life!"

"Hey, why's everybody mad at me?" Brian said, embarrassed. "I didn't do anything—"

"Shut up, Brian," Salvador said.

"*Shhh!*" someone called from across the room.

Brian blushed. "Sorry." He grabbed his jacket and backpack. "You guys probably need some privacy anyhow. I better go." Then he disappeared out the door.

"Brian, wait up!" Elizabeth called after him.

"Fine," I cried, gathering up my things. "I guess we aren't going to do the stupid 'zine after all," I said, shoving past Elizabeth. "I don't think I could stand to see any of you ever again!"

Salvador

"Bienvenue en France!" someone announced behind me.

Elizabeth and I stared at each other across the language-lab table.

The look in her eyes told me everything.

I was a total jerk.

She hated me.

Things couldn't possibly be any worse—I had to try to make them better.

"I guess I messed things up pretty badly, didn't I?" I said at last.

But Elizabeth shook her head and sighed. "It wasn't just you, Salvador."

She pulled up a chair and sat down. "I've been a bad friend to Anna." She glanced up. "And to you."

"You mean you don't hate me?" I said, totally awestruck. I felt like kneeling down and kissing Elizabeth's feet.

But I had done enough kissing for the time being. I stayed where I was.

"No, I don't hate you," she said, looking down

at her hands. "I was kind of mad at you at first, I guess. I mean, things were kind of confusing. . . ."

"You're telling me," I muttered.

"But the weirdest thing was that I didn't know how to act around either of you anymore."

"I know the feeling," I said. I ran a hand through my hair. "Getting together with Anna— it was all a mistake. She was so upset that day I went to see her. I wanted to make her feel better." I laughed bitterly. "Instead I wound up making her hate me."

Elizabeth studied me with her intense blue-green eyes.

"You know what's funny?" she said at last.

Funny? I couldn't think of anything. "What?"

Elizabeth smiled sadly. "Anna hates us, but *we* thought we were doing all this for *her*. And right now, she wouldn't even believe us if we told her that."

I nodded. "Yeah, I know."

"I wish we could go back and redo everything. I just want us all to be friends again."

I smiled at her. I knew it hadn't been easy for her to say that. But I was so glad she had.

"Me too," I said.

We didn't say any more. It's kind of hard to talk about that kind of stuff without sounding like a dork. Especially in the language lab—even though everyone else was wearing headphones, they were probably all listening.

But I think Elizabeth and I both knew that we were going to try to fix everything so we could be friends again.

The romance stuff? There wasn't any room for it right now. Maybe later, if things worked out . . . But I wasn't going to think about that now. I was just glad that I had a really sweet, really cool, and really smart friend like Elizabeth.

I'd have to forget that she was the most beautiful girl I'd ever seen.

And we still had to make up with Anna. That is, if she ever gave us a chance.

Bethel

"Hey, Bethel, how was school?" Renee asked when I came home. She was sprawled on the sofa in the den, reading the newspaper and drinking chocolate milk with a straw. She sucked hard on the straw, but there were only a few drops of milk left, and it made that horrible phlegmy noise. How come she was only disgusting when we were alone together? Why didn't she do that sort of thing at one of her awards dinners so everyone would know what a pig she was?

She yawned and stretched, flopping back into the cushions. "I have done absolutely nothing today except run ten miles and eat and sleep. I love it."

I turned and headed for the stairs.

"Fine!" Renee shouted after me. "Ignore me!"

I stopped and retraced my steps. "What else do you want me to say?" I asked, leaning against the door frame. "School was awesome. I had a fight with Jessica, and I failed my math test because I wasn't prepared. Satisfied? It's really not that interesting."

"What'd you guys fight about?" Renee asked, sitting up and licking chocolate from the rim of the glass.

"None of your business," I said, crossing my arms.

"A boy?" she asked, smiling mischievously.

"Yeah, right," I scoffed.

"What was it, then? Jessica's really cool—why are you fighting with her?"

"Oh, right away it's my fault," I said. Renee was so predictable.

"Well, you storm around all the time like you're just waiting for a fight. What's wrong, Bethel?"

I stared at my sister, lying on the sofa, the newspaper spread around her like it was Sunday morning. A queen relaxing on her throne. She really had no clue.

"You know what's wrong with me?" I said. "*You*, that's what. And no, I don't want to talk about it. Particularly not with you." I turned and ran up the stairs, slamming the door to my room and hurling myself on my bed.

I knew I was acting like a rotten little kid. But that's what she wanted, wasn't it? And Renee *always* got what she wanted.

Elizabeth

I was sitting on my bed, trying to do my Spanish homework But the words were all running into each other.

Maybe I need glasses, I thought.

But how could I keep my mind on homework when Anna was out there somewhere hating me?

I had tried to be her friend by swearing to never speak to Salvador again. But even when I did it, I knew I didn't mean it. If I had been a *real* friend, I would have told Anna the truth.

I was a liar.

I didn't deserve a friend like Anna.

But I wanted her to be my friend again more than anything.

Plus I was really depressed about *Zone*.

How did everything get so messed up? I wondered in despair.

The whole idea of *Zone* had been so cool and exciting. And it had been so much fun working on it together. I couldn't believe that the whole thing was falling apart right before the first issue came out. It could have been so good.

The phone rang, but I didn't move. Someone picked it up after the first ring.

"Hey, Elizabeth!" my brother, Steven, shouted from downstairs. "It's for you."

Maybe it's Anna, calling to talk! I thought excitedly. "Who is it?" I called back.

"I don't know," Steven hollered. "Some guy."

I flew through the bathroom that connected my room to Jessica's. We shared a phone that had a cord long enough to drag back and forth between our rooms. As usual, it was in her room.

Jessica was trying on clothes and making two piles, one of clothes she wanted to keep and one of clothes she wanted to give away. She has this theory that if you give away lots of old clothes, you're entitled to buy lots of new clothes. When I came in, she had on a pair of black velvet leggings and a light blue, cropped sweater and was examining her bare stomach in the mirror. She whirled around self-consciously when she saw me.

"Liz!" she cried, annoyed.

I ignored her completely.

My heart was pounding as I reached for the phone. Was it Salvador? Maybe he'd had a chance to talk to Anna. . . . I snatched up the receiver. "Hello?" I said hopefully.

"Hi, Elizabeth."

For a moment I couldn't place the voice. It definitely wasn't Salvador.

"This is Brian—from school?"

"Oh. Hi, Brian," I answered, unable to hide my disappointment. He was about the last person I had expected to call, especially after this afternoon. I started to drag the phone back through the bathroom and into my room as he talked.

"Listen," Brian said. "I'm really sorry about today. You know, for opening my big mouth."

"That's okay," I said. "I mean, we were all kind of . . . emotional."

"Well, I felt like a lot of it was my fault," he said. "And I'm sorry."

"Thanks," I said.

I thought he might just hang up then. But he lingered. There was definitely something else on his mind.

"Brian?" I asked.

"Um . . . there's another problem," he said. "It's about *Zone*."

"You mean the now nonexistent alternative 'zine *Zone*?" I joked.

"Yeah, that's exactly what I mean," Brian said. "Remember all the money we raised selling ads?"

"Oh no." I groaned and flopped down on my bed. I'd forgotten all about that! "Well, I guess we'll just have to give it all back."

"We can't," Brian said.

"We can't?" I exclaimed, sitting up. "Why not?"

"Because," Brian explained, "we spent almost all of it on supplies and promotional materials. If we don't publish the 'zine—including the ads we promised our sponsors—and earn back the money, we'll have to pay the sponsors back out of our own pockets."

My pockets weren't very full at the moment. That "little party" Jessica and I had thrown not long before had pretty much used up all my funds.

"How much is it?" I asked.

"Almost five hundred dollars."

"No way!" I shrieked. "That's a lot even if we split it four ways."

"I know," Brian agreed.

"Brian, what are we going to do?"

"I really don't know," Brian said despondently. If only we could still publish the 'zine. If only . . .

Hey, wait a minute, I thought. *Why can't we?* We had most of the first issue put together. There wasn't much else left to do.

But the question was: Did we still have a staff to do it?

"Brian," I said, "there's only one thing to do."

"I thought of that," Brian said. "But I decided a bank robbery wouldn't look too good on my record. I kind of want to go to college."

I laughed out loud. "It's nothing that drastic."

"Good!" he said, sounding more cheerful. "So, what's your idea?"

"We'll just have to publish *Zone*—whether we're all friends or not."

"Wow," Brian said. "I don't know. I don't think Salvador and Anna are talking to me."

"So?" I said. "People who work on real magazine staffs—or any real jobs—aren't always friends."

Brian chuckled. "Good point."

"So," I went on, "this will just be more like a real magazine. We'll have a *professional* relationship."

Brian laughed. "Only you could come up with that kind of reasoning."

"Besides," I added, "Salvador's pretty much over it already."

It was kind of a strange thing to say. I mean, I really didn't know whether Salvador was over me or Anna or how he really felt about anything.

I just knew that I was ready for us all to move on.

"What about Anna?" Brian asked.

I sighed. "I don't know. That may take some time."

"Do you really think we can pull it off?" Brian asked.

"We have to," I insisted. "Unless you want to have a really huge bake sale!"

"No way!" Brian said.

Elizabeth

I promised to call Anna and Salvador, and we said good-bye, laughing.

As soon as I hung up, I dialed Anna's number.

"Hello?" It was Anna's mother.

"This is Elizabeth Wakefield. May I speak to Anna, please?"

"I'm sorry," she said in a polite, distant voice. "Anna can't come to the phone right now. She's busy."

"Oh—well, will you tell her I called?" I asked.

"I'll give her the message."

"Tell her she can call me as late as nine-thirty—"

But she had already hung up.

Next I dialed Salvador's number.

"Hello?" the Doña answered.

"Hi," I said. "This is Elizabeth. May I speak to Salvador, please?"

"I'm so sorry," she said in a friendly voice. "He's out. But I'll tell him you called."

"Thank you," I said, and hung up.

Salvador was out this late on a school night?

Could he be at Anna's? Maybe that was why she was busy?

I could hardly stand not knowing.

You can't do anything about it now, I told myself.

After the emotional day I'd had, I needed to focus on something that had no feelings. I needed logic and order and cold, hard, dispassionate facts.

I needed to do my homework.

Instant Messages between Brian Rainey, Kristin Seltzer, and Lacey Frells

BRainE:	You looked really pretty today
Kgrl99:	Did not
BRainE:	Did so
Kgrl99:	Moving on to less embarrassing topics . . .
BRainE:	U r no good at taking compliments
Kgrl99:	but u r good at giving them
BRainE:	Kristin?
Kgrl99:	Brian?
BRainE:	There's something I want to ask
Kgrl99:	Ask away
L88er:	Hey boys and girls
Kgrl99:	Not now Lace
BRainE:	Hi Lacey
Kgrl99:	Brian?
L88er:	So Kristin you're coming to Gel's Friday right?
Kgrl99:	Lacey?
L88er:	Yes?
Kgrl99:	Like could you *leave* now, please?!

L88er:	Fine
Kgrl99:	I'll explain later
L88ter:	Ok—L8ter. Ha ha
Kgrl99:	Bye Lacey
Kgrl99:	Brian?
Kgrl99:	Brian?

Salvador

"You've reached the Wang residence." Anna's voice on the machine was adult and formal. "We're not available to take your call, so please leave a message after the tone." *Beep*.

"Anna, it's Salvador. I just want to say I feel terrible, and I'm so, so sorry . . . . I really want to talk to you. . . . I know you probably don't want to call me, though, so I'll just keep trying. I'm just really, really—"

Beep! The machine cut me off.

I slammed down the phone in frustration.

Anna's house was only a few blocks from mine.

I took the stairs two at a time and found the Doña watching championship wrestling in the living room.

"I'm just going over to Anna's for a sec," I announced.

I must have looked guilty, or worried, or something because the Doña glanced up at me suspiciously. "Are you in trouble, Salvador?" she asked.

"A little," I admitted.

"Do you want to tell me about it?" she offered, pressing the mute button on the remote.

I shrugged. "I think I'd better try and work things out for myself first," I answered. I appreciated her offer, but there were already more people involved than necessary (read: Brian). I went over and gave the Doña a little hug. "Thanks, though," I said.

"You're a good boy," she said, patting my shoulder. "When you give yourself half a chance."

Whatever that meant.

I headed for the door. "See you in a few," I told her.

The lights were on upstairs in Anna's room. Downstairs only the kitchen light was on.

I rang the doorbell once, twice. Nothing.

I waited. "Come on, Anna," I muttered to myself. Still nothing.

I rang the bell again and stepped back to look up at Anna's bedroom window. But I couldn't see anything.

I was about to turn around and head for home when the front door opened and Anna's mother appeared, clutching the collar of her bathrobe. Had I woken her up?

I felt kind of embarrassed.

110

"Hi," I said awkwardly. "Is Anna in?"

"Hello, Salvador," Mrs. Wang said, looking me up and down. "She's studying. You can talk to her in school tomorrow."

I didn't want to force my way in or yell or anything, but I was kind of expecting Mrs. Wang to at least tell Anna I was there and let Anna decide if she wanted to speak to me or not.

But she just closed the door.

And I felt even worse than I'd felt before.

Dear Renee,

I think it's important for us to be honest with each other.

I don't like you, and you don't like me. Just because we're sisters doesn't mean we have to be friends, right?

So let's just stop pretending.

Go back to college and leave me in peace.

Thank you.
Bethel

Forget it, there's no way I can give her this.

Elizabeth

The next day, before classes started, I searched for Salvador.

At last I spotted him, standing at the end of the hall, with sunlight streaming in the window behind him.

To my surprise, my heart did a little flip-flop. And for a moment I let myself enjoy that feeling.

Then I did something that felt right, if not exactly good. I took that feeling and tucked it away, like a love note hidden in a drawer.

Maybe one day I'd take it out again. But for now I had more urgent problems to solve. Like putting out a magazine. And saving two *very* important friendships.

"Salvador!" I hurried down the crowded hall to meet him.

Was it my imagination, or did his eyes light up when he saw me?

His smile was warm and friendly, not awkward, like it had been for over a week. I felt pretty sure that maybe he'd done the same kind of thing with his feelings that I'd done with mine. Tucked them away for another day.

And for now that felt just right.

"I tried to call you last night," I said.

"I know—the Doña told me. I went over to Anna's house to talk to her."

I bit my lip. "What happened? What did she say?"

Salvador shook his head. "Her mother said she was busy studying. I think she just didn't want to talk to me. I felt really bad, so I walked around for a while, and by the time I got home, I figured it was too late to call you."

He walked with me down the busy, crowded hall toward my locker. "So, what's up?"

"We've got a problem," I told him. "A big one."

"Why, what's wrong?" he asked, a worried look on his face.

"Brian called last night," I said.

"Oh, that." Salvador shook his head. "It wasn't his fault everything blew up at the 'zine meeting. It was bound to happen sometime. I'll catch up with him today and tell him everything's cool."

"But everything's not cool," I said.

"Why not?"

I told him all about Brian's phone call last

night: that if we didn't publish the magazine with our sponsors' ads, we'd have to give them all their money back.

Salvador grimaced. "Bummer. I hadn't thought of that. How much money is it exactly?" he asked.

"Five hundred dollars."

Salvador laughed out loud. "You're kidding."

I shook my head.

Salvador's smile disappeared. "You're *not* kidding?"

"No."

Salvador ran a nervous hand through his thick, dark hair and bit his lip. "Well, there's only one thing to do."

"What's that?" I asked, marveling at the fact that Salvador had managed to come up with a plan in a matter of seconds when I had been racking my brain all night.

"Rob a bank," Salvador joked.

I laughed. "That's exactly what Brian said."

"Great minds think alike, I guess."

"Seriously," I went on. "There's only one thing we really *can* do. We have to keep going and do the first issue, even if it's the only one we ever publish."

Salvador nodded. "Well, I'm up for it. And we've got most of an issue done anyway, right?"

"Right." I nodded. We'd reached my locker, and I fiddled with the combination. "And we could use the stuff we wrote that the *Spectator* rejected if we need to fill space."

My lock slipped free, and I swung open my locker. My cafeteria article—the one I'd written spoofing our school's gross cafeteria—was taped to the inside of the door. "Like this. I mean, *if* everybody likes it," I added hastily.

"Likes it?" Salvador said. "I love it. It's one of the funniest things I've ever read. The *Spectator* was crazy not to use it."

I glowed at his compliment. "Thanks. And what about your cartoons?"

He'd created a cartoon character named Wonder Girl—who actually looked a lot like me.

"If you don't mind," he said shyly. "I'd like to."

"Sure. They were really good."

Salvador held out his hands, and I handed him my backpack while I pulled out the books I'd need for my morning classes. "Brian wrote that movie review," he went on. "I'm sure he could do more."

I could tell Salvador was getting excited about working on *Zone* again. "That'd be great," I said. "And I'm sure Anna has tons of—"

I broke off.

Salvador and I stared at each other uneasily.

I knew he was thinking the same thing I was. Was there any way Anna would help us with the magazine now? Or would she just blow us off?

"I'm sure she has lots of poems," I said softly. "And I'm sure when she hears about the money and how much we all want to publish our work, she'll help us out. Even if she's still mad."

"I hope," Salvador said.

I closed my locker and spun the combination dial. "Salvador, we've got to talk to her. We've got to apologize."

"I know." Salvador handed me my backpack.

We looked up and down the hall, scanning the endless faces of milling, chattering students. Everyone seemed so happy. Didn't anybody else have any problems?

"I haven't seen her all morning," Salvador said. "Have you?"

"No." I sighed. "Maybe she's avoiding us."

"Don't worry," Salvador said. "I'll track her down. And I'll tell bad jokes until she promises to forgive us and be friends with us again!"

I smiled. Same old Salvador, always able to make you laugh.

But I couldn't help but think that there really wasn't anything to laugh about.

By the time Salvador and I met in the cafeteria for lunch, we'd found out where Anna was.

Home sick.

Salvador scooped up some applesauce and

117

stirred it into his mashed potatoes. "Like I really believe she's sick." He shook his head. "She's faking. She didn't even have a sniffle yesterday."

I stared at Salvador's lunch tray and the weird mess he was making on his plate. "Salvador, what are you *doing?*"

"You mean this?" Grinning, he scooped up a big spoonful and stuffed it in his mouth. "It's my—"

"It's okay; you can swallow first. I can wait."

He swallowed, then smiled. "Ahh. My favorite. If you eat it really fast, the mashed potatoes are still hot and the applesauce is still cold in your mouth. It's . . . awesome."

I shook my head, laughing. "You are so weird!"

"No, I'm not! Try it!" He shoved a spoonful toward me.

"No way!" I shrieked, covering my mouth and scooting back.

"The Doña made it up for me when I was little," he said. "I wouldn't eat her mashed potatoes. So she mixed in some applesauce. I know it looks gross, but I liked it. Mashed potatoes just don't taste right without it."

I rolled my eyes. That was Salvador all over. Just a little bit weird. And lots of fun.

Then I remembered Anna, and I felt a little

guilty. Here I was having fun with her best friend when she was home feeling miserable.

"Salvador, what are we going to do?" I asked.

His eyes sobered, remembering our problem. He stirred his mashed-potato-applesauce goop without eating. "I don't know. All of this . . . with us, and everything with her brother . . . She's gotta be feeling low," Salvador said. He shoved his tray aside, his chair scraping noisily as he got up. "I'll be right back. I'm going to try to call her."

"But what if she doesn't answer the phone?" I asked. "What if she won't talk to you?"

Salvador's usually smiling mouth was set in a determined, straight line. "Then we'll just go over there and ring the doorbell and knock on the door. . . ."

"And throw pebbles at her window," I put in.

"And blast her house with loud, heavy-metal music like the police do . . . until she goes nuts and lets us in!"

We both laughed.

But our laughter couldn't erase the worried look in our eyes.

I stayed at the table, nibbling on my sandwich, not really hungry, oblivious to the usual lunchtime craziness that swirled around me.

Elizabeth

Suddenly I realized someone was standing in front of me. I looked up.

"Oh, hi, Brian." I smiled.

He pulled a chair around backward and sat down, his arms resting on the chair back. "So, what's the verdict? Is *Zone* going to happen or what?"

"Yes," I said firmly. "But you might have to count Anna out."

Brian grimaced. "I noticed she wasn't in history today. You don't think she's really sick, do you?"

"Uh-uh. Salvador just went to try and call her," I explained. "Maybe he can talk to her." I shrugged. "Either way, I still want to do *Zone*."

"Me too," Brian said. He smiled and stood up. "I'll see if I can catch up with Salvador. Talk to you later."

Minutes later Salvador came back.

"I saw Brian," he said.

"Everything okay?" I asked.

"Yeah, he's really excited about doing the 'zine again." Then he added, "Nobody answers at Anna's house."

I stared at him. "Well, do you think it's because no one's there? Or no one's answering?"

"Hard to tell. The answering machine comes

on. She could just be screening me out."

I offered Salvador my chocolate pudding, and he instantly made it disappear.

The bell rang, signaling the end of lunch.

"Meet me after school?" Salvador asked, gathering up our trays.

I nodded.

"We're going over there, and we're going to *make* her talk to us," he said.

The Wangs' TV

"—on today's show, girlfriends get back at their exes!"

Click!

"But Brad! What if Marsha finds out? And what if Sylvia tells Eric about what Marsha found in her twin sister Natasha's room? And what if Natasha—"

Click!

"—even stubborn grass stains—even *pepperoni pizza* stains—come out with new, improved, liquid—"

Click!

"Oh, Brad—"

Click!

"Coming up next—a recipe for fish so low in fat, you can have seconds or even—"

Click!

"And now to the White House, where Lucy Stone

is standing by for the president's press conference on—"

Click!

"—genuine zirconium diamonds! Let's see if we can get a close-up. There we go! Aren't they gorgeous? But better hurry. There are only a limited number of these left in our warehouse. And if you order within the next five minutes, you can split your payment into three easy installments—"

Click!

"Captain Muscle has Han Hangman in a headlock. He's going down! One, two, three . . .

Click!

Bethel

Jessica and I shared the last class of the day—history. A guest speaker from the university was lecturing about the fall of the Berlin Wall, and Mr. Harriman had warned us to be on our best behavior. Jessica was sitting only one desk away, but I kept my eyes forward, glued to the speaker's mouth.

I'm not avoiding her, I told myself. *I'm being a good student.*

Mr. Harriman usually let us out a few minutes early when we had a track meet, and when the clock clicked to the hour, I was out the door before he could even open his mouth to say anything. Or maybe he didn't even notice. I'm pretty fast, and I know how to be quiet.

I dressed in my SVJH blue-and-silver uniform and hit the track before anyone else showed up, even Coach Krebs.

It was a beautiful day. The air smelled crisp and clean, and the sun felt good on my face.

A stiff breeze blew, tumbling an empty Doritos bag across the track. I jogged over and snatched it up, tossing it into a trackside trash can.

I started my warm-ups and began psyching myself up for the meet ahead.

I knew I was a good runner. And I always wanted to win.

But I never assumed I would be the best runner at a meet. I always counted on someone showing up who would test me, push me to the limits of my ability.

I'd win as long as I kept my head clear and didn't think about fighting with Renee. Or Jessica.

Stop it, I told myself. Negative thoughts could ruin a run.

And today I felt like running like I'd never run before.

All too soon my moments of privacy were stolen away by other girls coming out onto the track and then by the rival bus pulling into the parking lot and spitting out a bunch of girls in green-and-white uniforms.

I shaded my eyes against the sun and watched the other girls coming onto the track, scoping them out, looking for long legs, swaggers, signs of who might be their top runner.

Behind me I heard footsteps jogging toward

me on the track. I knew it was Jessica before I even turned around.

"Hey, Bethel!" she said, her blue-green eyes hopeful and guarded all at once.

I started to turn away. I really didn't feel like talking to her. I didn't want to get in a bad mood right before a race.

"Bethel, wait—" She caught me by the arm. I stared at her hand, and she let it drop. "I'm really sorry about everything. Whatever I did to make you mad at me. Okay?"

I shrugged. What did she want me to say?

Jessica put her hands on her hips and glared at me. "Bethel McCoy. You're going to quit acting like an idiot or I'm going to . . . to . . ."

I raised an eyebrow. "What?"

"I'll . . . I'll trip you!"

I burst out laughing. Jessica looked like a little girl picking a fight on the playground. "What? You don't want me in your sandbox unless I'm going to play nice?"

Jessica grinned, then said seriously, "Bethel, I didn't mean to interfere with anything going on with your sister. And I really hate when you ignore me."

I swallowed.

"And I really do know what it's like living with a perfect sister," she went on. "Believe me, there's just no point in trying to compete. The only way to deal with it is just to be yourself."

I rolled my eyes. "Thanks for the Hallmark greeting, Jess."

"Oh, come on," Jessica said, and punched me on the arm. "I'm trying to be nice—I know I sound like a dork."

I laughed. I couldn't help it. And suddenly I just didn't feel mad at her anymore. She was too good a friend.

"I think you're very cool, Bethel," she said. "Who cares about your sister?" Then she smiled at me. "Now, can we just go back to being friends? How am I going to be a famous track star if you won't help me out?"

"You, a track star?" I said, teasing. "Girl, you have a long way to go—"

"*Run,*" she corrected me.

"A long way to *run* before you can even *dream* about being a track star."

"Oh yeah?" Jessica said. "Then I guess it's a good thing I've got you to chase."

"Yeah, I guess it is," I said cockily.

And then it hit me.

Was I chasing Renee?

Was I somehow better than I otherwise would have been if she hadn't been there—ahead of me—my whole life?

Did I run faster, get better grades, push myself because I'd been chasing my big sister ever since I'd taken my first step?

The thought blew me away.

Maybe Renee wasn't so bad after all.

But there was time to think about that later. Because now, we had some serious running to do.

Jessica was staring at me. "So, what's going on in that crazy head of yours?" she asked me.

"Wakefield," I said in my best jock voice, "you're all right."

She laughed. "See if you still say that at the end of the meet!" she challenged.

"In your dreams!" I hooted.

Laughing, we jogged over to where Coach Krebs was gathering our team for her usual big pep talk.

". . . and if you ladies can catch a little of Bethel's magic footwork, we might just leave our opponents eating our dust today," the coach said as we approached.

Jessica nudged me, grinning, and I nudged her back. My teammates weren't judging me against anyone else's standards—they were setting their sights on *me*. It was a great feeling.

When we finally hit the starting line, I took a deep breath and gazed up at the sky. As my gaze dropped, my eyes crossed the bleachers, which were nearly empty compared to the crowds at our football games.

But there was one spectator sitting all alone, high in the stands, waving at me.

My sister. Renee.

She waved again and shouted something at me. I couldn't hear, but I guessed it was something to cheer me on.

Catch me if you can! I imagined her shouting—both a cheer and a challenge.

I waved back. "Watch me!" I called, although I knew she couldn't hear what I said.

I jogged over to the starting line and crouched down, my knees bent low, weight forward, eyes set on the course ahead of me.

And when the referee said the familiar words, "Ready, set, *go!*" and fired the cap gun, I ran like I'd finally been set free.

A n n a

I'd never skipped out on a day of school in my life. In elementary school I always got a little certificate at the last assembly each year for not missing a single day.

Playing sick was easy now. All I had to do was sniffle, and my mom was all over me, worried, taking my temperature, and forcing fluids till I thought I'd throw up for real.

But staying home was boring. And being smothered by a mother who was a professional nurse was even worse than being in school with back-stabbing friends.

The attention she was giving me now was manic and obsessive . . . like in some demented way she was trying to reach Tim through me.

I hated it.

Dad had made me tea with honey and lemon before he left for work. Then my mother came downstairs and started taking my temperature and bringing me blankets and sitting by my feet and staring at me.

I finally got rid of her by asking her to make Grandma's special spicy soup.

Mom was so delighted to be suddenly given a mission, she raced off to the market to buy the ingredients.

"And maybe some chocolate-vanilla-swirl frozen yogurt from Yummy Yogurts?" I had called to her in the hall. "It's my favorite." Adding another stop to her shopping trip would keep her out of the house even longer.

When she left, I curled up on the couch under the afghan my grandmother had knitted for me when I was little. The phone rang, but I didn't feel like moving from the couch. I let the answering machine take the call.

After the beep I heard Salvador's voice, calling me from school: "Anna, are you there? Pick up! Hello? Can you hear me? I heard you were home sick. Are you okay? Yo! Hel-lo? . . . I'll wait a minute so you can get to the phone. . . . One, one thousand; two, one thousand. Zip-a-dee-doo-dah! Zip-a-dee-ay!" he sang. Then he started whistling.

Only Salvador . . . , I thought, shaking my head with a smile.

But I didn't pick up.

I heard him sigh. "Well, I guess you're delirious with fever or something. I'll try you again later. Feel better. Byee!"

Anna

I turned back to the TV. Once again I started flipping through the three-hundred-some channels that the satellite dish fed daily into our house.

Cartoons, home-decorating shows, news channels, soap operas, talk shows with creepy guests.

I clicked over to the cartoon channel. Maybe watching some cats and dogs hitting each other over the head with clubs and getting run over by steamrollers would cheer me up.

I watched a few minutes until the dog and cat teamed up and started chasing the mouse. That's when I gave it up and finally clicked off the set.

I pulled the afghan up over my head and stared at the ceiling through the little holes. Each square in the pattern was crocheted with different colors of yarn.

When we were little, Tim and I played all kinds of games with that afghan. Laying the afghan across chairs to make a fort. Curling up under it to watch TV when we both had the chicken pox, laughing and crying at the same time when the yarn made us itch even more.

A huge lump rose in my throat, making me feel like I was going to choke. Almost a year later and the sadness was just as strong . . . worse even, because I'd had time for it to sink in. What seemed at first impossible was a truth that would never change. I no longer woke up thinking it might have been a dream or a mistake.

Tim was dead, and he was never coming back. *Just give me back my brother!* I felt like shouting. But there was nothing anyone could do.

I cried for a while, hiding under that multi-colored afghan like a little girl afraid of monsters. With no big brother to come and make the scary shadows disappear.

Then I got up and went into the bathroom to blow my nose and wash my face.

I dried my face on a fluffy blue towel and stared out the bathroom window into our back-yard, at the tree house where Tim and I used to play. How many times had we scrambled up the rope ladder to hide in that scrap-wood house from pirates and wild animals?

"Ahoy, matey!" Tim would shout in his goofy, made-up British accent, gazing through the tele-scope we made from a cardboard paper-towel roll. "Danger ahead!"

I buried my face in the towel and started to cry once more.

If only I could have seen the danger ahead for Tim . . . if only I could have done something. If I'd gone with him in the car that night, maybe I could have jerked the wheel and steered us out of that drunk's path. Maybe *I* could have been the one to die instead of Tim.

Anna

I need you, big brother, I cried into the towel. And just then I knew where I needed to go.

I scribbled a note to my mom on the family marker board beside the fridge and ran out the door.

Elizabeth

"Salvador, where are you?" I mumbled nervously, pacing back and forth in front of Sweet Valley Junior High's main entrance.

I'd been waiting out front until everyone was gone but the stragglers, kids waiting for moms who were always running a little late.

The vice principal had even come out and taken down the flag.

"Elizabeth!"

I whirled around to see Salvador running toward me.

"Where were you?" I asked.

"Sorry," he said, catching his breath. "Ms. Martine insisted that I stay after for a few minutes so she could talk to me about next month's Math Bowl."

"That sounds like a good time," I joked.

He laughed. "That's what I get for being a math genius." His grin faded. "So, ready to go?"

I nodded. "I'm kind of dreading it a little."

"I know," Salvador said as we started walking.

Elizabeth

"It's not going to be fun. But don't worry."

He smiled, and instantly I felt better.

We didn't talk much on the walk over, and it was nice. You know you're really friends with someone when you don't have to talk all the time.

When we got to Anna's house, we stopped out on the sidewalk and stared up at the window of her room on the second floor.

"It sure would be nice if I could skip this part and get right to the good part where we all hug and make up," Salvador said.

I pushed him toward the Wangs' front door. "Come on, Sal. Let's get this over with."

We walked up the steps. "The house seems really quiet," I said.

"The Wang house is *always* quiet," Salvador said. He stepped up to the front door and rang the bell.

We waited a respectable length of time, and then Salvador rang it again.

Ding-ding, ding-ding, ding-ding, ding—

"Salvador!" I said, pulling his hand off the doorbell.

"Hey, if her mom or dad was home, they'd have answered the door already," he said. "If Anna's in there, I want her to know I'm not leaving till she comes to the door."

Ding-ding, ding-ding, ding-ding . . .

But after a few more rings even Salvador gave up.

"I don't think she's in there," Salvador said.

"Maybe she fell asleep with headphones on," I suggested, but I knew it sounded lame.

"What if she's really sick?" Salvador said, looking worried. "What if it's something serious—and they had to take her to the doctor?"

"Calm down," I reassured him. But I couldn't help it. I was worried too.

Maybe she just really, really doesn't want to talk to us, I thought.

We waited for a few more minutes in case *somebody* changed their mind and opened the door. But nobody ever did.

Instant Messages between Brian Rainey and Kristin Seltzer

Kgrl99: You wanted to ask me something yesterday?

BRainE: I think it will be better to ask in person

Kgrl99: Pleeaase?

BRainE: The longer u wait, the better it will be

Kgrl99: Ooo sometimes u can be sooo—

BRainE: cute?

BRainE: adorable?

BRainE: perfect?

BRainE: Kristin?

Kgrl99: I'll see you "in person"

BRainE: I'll be there

A n n a

I hadn't been there in almost a year.

Not since the day we buried Tim.

It was a nice place, as cemeteries go, I guess. They kept the grass mowed. Most of the people brought real flowers, not just those gross plastic ones. Elegant benches invited visitors to sit beneath the trees and meditate on questions of eternity. They even locked the gates at night so kids couldn't come in and steal the flowers or knock over the headstones.

But ever since the funeral, I had refused to come and "visit Tim," as my mother liked to say. Refused to go with her to lay fresh flowers on the gravestone of a person who couldn't smell them, who couldn't see his mother's tears drop onto the fresh, green grass covering the ground where he lay.

I had stood by my parents during the funeral, as still as one of the angel statues silently guarding some of the other graves.

And my heart had felt as if it had turned to

stone. I didn't even cry. That didn't come till later.

Even then I'd refused to think of him . . . down there . . . stuffed into some polished wood box lined with overpriced satin and bows.

It wasn't him.

It wasn't real.

I wouldn't believe it!

The day had been a lot like today. The colors had been almost surreal, so bright in the crisp October air as the sun kept trying to break through, only to be overcome by thick chunks of clouds, which turned everything gray.

Sunshine and shadow.

Yin and yang.

But there were no smiles to balance out the tears that day. Only pain and sorrow.

It was a little gusty, and the wind kept blowing my hair across my face and eyes, as if to say, *Don't look, don't look.*

Tears began to stream down my face as I stood there, my hands stuffed into my pockets. And then . . .

Suddenly I was on my knees beside his gravestone, talking to him. The words poured out like the time when he'd come home after a month at summer camp and I'd had so much to tell him.

I don't even know what I was saying—the words almost seemed to flow out of my mouth on their own. But I had been so lonely, it felt good to just spill my guts. I'm not sure how much I said aloud and how much I only thought in my heart.

And then, at last, the words and tears ended, like a bucket that had poured out all its water.

I sat back on my heels and wiped the sleeve of my jacket across my eyes.

I knew that wasn't *really* my brother lying down there underground in the fancy box, beneath the headstone with his name formally engraved on it. But I felt close to him, as I hadn't felt since he left us.

My brother was with me.

I looked up across the grounds as a big, black car drove up. The driver got out and helped a small, bent old woman out of the car. He started to walk with her, but she pulled away from him.

Clutching a cane and small bouquet of lilies, the woman walked toward a row of huge, showy marble headstones—

She passed them and at last stopped at a small, heart-shaped stone about two feet high.

With great effort she placed the flowers at the

foot of the stone, using her cane to push herself back up. Then she just stood there.

Watching the old woman, I couldn't help but wonder if I would still be coming to see Tim when I was old and bent.

Would I still cry?

Would I ever be all right again?

Would I ever get over feeling guilty for still being here—while Tim had been cheated out of the rest of his life?

I looked back down at the grass on Tim's grave, and I don't know why I thought of it, but I suddenly remembered a big picnic we'd gone to when we were little.

I was in a sack race, and halfway to the finish line I fell down.

I was only about five, and I started crying. I wanted to quit the race and sit back down with my parents. But Tim was there on the sidelines. He ran up to me and said, "You can't quit, Anna. You've gotta keep running. You've gotta stay in the race."

"But I can't win now," I cried.

"Who cares?" he said, helping me up. "Just keep going for yourself."

So I pulled up my sack and started hopping again.

I didn't win, of course. By the time I finished,

the other kids had met up with their families and were going off to other activities.

But Tim was there, waiting for me at the finish line with open arms. And when I reached him, he picked me up and shouted, "All right, Anna!"

I miss him so much!

And that's when I realized. There *was* something I could do for Tim.

I could get up and keep going.

I couldn't give Tim his life back. But I could live my life—for me *and for him.*

And for the first time in days I felt a calmness come over me. Not happiness, exactly. But a feeling of peace.

I walked to the side of Tim's grave and traced his name in the headstone with my fingertips.

Tim would want me to be happy. That was something I could do for him.

He'd want me to take care of Mom too, I thought, and I felt ashamed of how angry I'd been with her. I would try to do better at that too.

Life was too precious to waste time being angry at people who loved you.

Maybe I *would* go to a therapist. But I would ask Mom and Dad to go with me. Maybe that way we could find a way to talk about all this together. And try to be a real family again.

I knew my brother would like that.

Anna

"I love you, Tim," I whispered.

Then I stood up and hurried down the path out of the cemetery.

I felt so much better. I couldn't wait to tell someone how good I felt!

And I knew just who I wanted to tell.

Elizabeth

The doorbell rang, and I nearly spilled my Coke.

I was pretty sure it couldn't be Anna. But still . . .

I ran to the door, with Salvador right behind me.

I yanked it open.

And there was Anna, her eyes red from crying. But she had a big smile on her face.

Nobody said anything. For a split second I was worried that she might misinterpret Salvador's presence at my house. Worried that she might misread the whole situation.

But then Anna threw her arms around both of us. I was so surprised, I didn't know what to say. So I just hugged her back. I was so relieved, I started laughing and kind of crying at the same time. Salvador was laughing too.

Then Anna pulled away. "Can I come in?" she asked, wiping her nose with the back of her hand.

"Oh—sure!" I said, pulling her in. Salvador shut the door behind us, and I led us all into the living room.

We piled onto the couch, me and Salvador on either side of Anna.

"I just wanted to tell you both that I'm sorry," Anna said.

"*You're* sorry?" Salvador said. "Hey, we're the ones who are sorry—"

"Shut up, Sal, and let me talk!" Anna interrupted, bonking him with a pillow.

"Help me, Elizabeth!" Salvador cried, covering his face with his arms. "She's got a black belt in pillow fighting!"

We started giggling and whacking each other with pillows. It felt so good to be kidding around again, relaxed and easy, just like old times.

"Seriously," Anna said. "I'm not sure how everything got so mixed up—except I think Sal had a lot to do with it!" She whacked him with the pillow again.

"Ow, no fair!" Salvador said, fending her off.

"We were worried about you today," I said in a serious tone. "We stopped by after school, and no one was home."

Anna took a deep breath and smiled. "I went to Tim's grave."

I gasped. I didn't mean to, but I was surprised.

Salvador reached for her hand. "Anna—"

"No, it's okay, really," Anna said. "I needed to go. And it made me think about stuff. Like how much I'd miss you guys if I really never spoke to you again."

We were all quiet for a moment, thinking about that. There was something about Anna's voice now. A confidence that hadn't been there before. It made me think that maybe things weren't so bad after all.

"So," Anna said at last, "what else is new?"

I laughed.

Then Salvador told her about the situation with *Zone*—how we needed to get the 'zine out there or go broke.

"So, are you in, Anna?" Salvador asked.

"Are you kidding?" she said. "Of course I'm in. Doing the 'zine with you guys is one of the coolest things I've ever done. It's going to be great. And the next issue is going to be even better."

We hadn't really been talking about going beyond this first issue after everything had fallen apart. But now that we were working things out, *Zone* might have a long and happy life.

Then I had a really amazing idea. I hoped Anna would think so too.

"I have a suggestion," I announced.

Anna elbowed Salvador on the arm. "The

147

staff's back together five minutes, and she's already trying to run. things," she teased. "So, what's the big idea?"

"I think we should dedicate our first issue to your brother."

Anna sucked in her breath, and tears glistened in her eyes. I wasn't sure if that was a good sign or not.

Then she gave me a huge hug. "That's so sweet," she said, her voice thick with emotion. Then she sat back up. "Is it okay with you, Sal?"

"You bet," he said. "And I'm sure Brian will think so too."

"Okay, then," Anna said, smiling. "Thanks."

"*Zone* is going to be awesome," I said.

"Awesome?" Salvador exclaimed. "No way. It's going to blow the *Spectator* completely away!"

Just then Jessica burst in the front door, whooping and cheering and carrying three huge Vito's pizza boxes. Bethel came right in behind her, carrying two six-packs of soda and shouting at the top of her lungs, followed by an older girl who looked a lot like Bethel, who was also whooping and cheering.

"Hey, everybody!" Jessica said. "This is Bethel's sister, Renee." Then she started whooping again.

"What happened?" I shouted over the noise. "What's going on?"

"The track meet!" Jessica shouted. "We totally won! Bethel ran her fastest time ever!"

"I had to," Bethel said, laughing. "Your sister here was just *inches* behind me."

"No way," Jessica argued happily. "I think it was at least two feet!"

"You better watch these girls," Renee said, putting her arms around Jessica and Bethel like a proud coach. "They're going places."

Salvador and Anna and I clapped for our winning athletes and then helped them rip open the pizza boxes.

"Hey, maybe we could interview you and the team for *Zone*," Anna suggested. "Elizabeth—quick! Do you have something I can write with? I want to interview them while they're still pumped!"

I jumped up and hurried to find Anna a pen and some paper.

When I came back, Salvador was loading Anna's slice up with pepperoni and she was tossing olives into his mouth one at a time.

I was so happy to see that they were friends again, I didn't even care if they got pizza on the floor.

ZONE DEDICATION

This first issue of *Zone*
is dedicated to
Tim Wang,
a good brother and a good friend.
His laughter will be missed.
His love will never be forgotten.

Check out the **all-new**....

Sweet Valley Web site—

www.sweetvalley.com

New Features

Cool Prizes

the
ONLY
official
Web site!

Hot Links

And much more!